I0779978

For the Love of Dogs

June Whyte

A Gumshoe Chicks Mystery
Book 2

White City

Press

Books by June Whyte

Sex on Tuesdays

THE GUMSHOE CHICK MYSTERY SERIES
Gone to the Dogs
For the Love of Dogs
Doggone It!

VETS 2U MYSTERY SERIES
Murder at Kangaroo Downs
Death at Dingo Creek
Homicide at Emu Lodge

KAT MCKINLEY GREYHOUND MYSTERIES
Chasing Can Be Murder
Muzzled
Hounded
Leashed

CHIANA RYAN CHILDREN'S MYSTERIES
The Case of the Disappearing Corpse
The Case of the Missing Dinosaur Egg

www.amazon.com/author/junewhytebooks

For the Love of Dogs

✳✳

June Whyte

This edition published by White City Press
An imprint of Misti Media LLC
https://www.mistimedia.com
Available in both Paperback and eBook Editions
1 2 3 4 5 6 7 8 9 10
Text Copyright © June Whyte 2020
Paperback ISBN: 9781963479195
eBook ISBN: 9781963479102

Without limiting the rights under copyright reserved above, no part of this publication may be reproduced, stored in or introduced into a retrieval system, or transmitted, in any form, or by any means (electronic, mechanical, photocopying, recording, or otherwise), without the prior written permission of both the copyright owners and the above publisher of this book.

The scanning, uploading, and distribution of this book via the Internet or via any other means without the permission of the publisher is illegal and punishable by law. Please purchase only authorized electronic editions, and do not participate in or encourage electronic piracy of copyrighted materials. Your support of the author's rights is appreciated.

For my family.

1

"Bad dog, Busta!" I eyeballed the show-judge's suede, postbox red, ribbed, knee-high boots with the round toes and platform soles. The *ruined* knee-high boots with the round toes and platform soles. "I'm so sorry." Face hotter than a bushfire in summer, I tugged on Busta's lead to bring him to heel. But it was too late. The damage was already done. My show dog, *Sir Willoughby of Cornwall*, Busta to his friends, had cocked his leg on the judge's eye-catching red boots – and immediately drained the swamp.

And it was all my fault. Me, Molly Jayne Gibson – romance writer and perpetual day-dreamer.

Instead of concentrating on setting my fox terrier up for the judge's appraisal, my mind had wandered to my latest romance, my work-in-progress, *Three's A Crowd*. In it, the two love interests, Gray and Tabitha, weren't co-operating at all. You see, although Gray was all for hopping into bed and getting on with it, Tabitha, who'd been left at the altar by Gray's best friend, Ethan, wasn't so easily convinced. In fact, nothing I suggested was changing Tabitha's mind. Not that I could blame her. Three hours earlier, she'd been dumped by a man she thought was the love of her life and Gray, who'd rescued her, was now being an insensitive A-hole. Yep. And I needed to do something about that too.

Meanwhile, back in the real world, by allowing Busta to express his opinion of the fifty-something show-judge, also, the Mayor's wife, I had embarrassed myself, big time.

"My God, these boots cost me a bomb. They're Gucci, for Christ's sake." Dressed in a too-short-for-her-age red mini and makeup layered on with a paint roller, Lady Hamilton-Davies wobbled two steps backwards while pointing an accusatory finger at the now butter-wouldn't-melt-in-his-mouth, Busta. "Get that beast away from me!"

"I'm sorry, I don't know what came over him. Honestly. He's not normally like this." I dug in my pocket for some tissues to wipe the woman's boots, but all I could find was a packet of gum, a small notebook and a biro. "Would you like me to put your shoes under the tap? Give them a bit of a scrub? Maybe I can wash away the stains."

"Under. The. Tap?" The woman's mouth opened so wide I discovered she'd never had a tonsillectomy. "Are you insane? These boots cost me more than you'd earn in a month."

As I averaged around $2000 a week writing sizzling hot romance novels, I seriously doubted that statement. But said nothing. Instead, I let out a deep sigh. To say the judge was unhappy, was like saying spiders enjoyed being splattered to death with a sledge hammer. Naturally, I'd recompense the woman for the damaged footwear, buy her a new pair, but ohmygod, I'd never live this embarrassment down. The day Molly Gibson let her dog, Busta, pee on the judge's shoes, would be a permanent fixture on the show grape-vine. I only prayed some smart entrepreneur hadn't used their phone to video the event and already downloaded it onto Facebook where it would quickly go viral.

From the corner of my eye, I could see the smirk on my opponent's face. Busta was up against the winning female fox terrier for the Best in Breed sash. And by the smug expression on the dog's face, it was almost like *Miss Moppet* knew she'd won the award. She stood straighter, adjusted her head to present her good side and lifted her stumpy tail higher. However, the dog's owner, one hand covering her mouth, shoulders shaking in suppressed laughter, was demonstrating exactly how much ribbing I would need to endure before Busta's little party trick was forgotten.

"Here!" The judge snatched a wide blue satin sash from the table and tossed it in the direction of the posing *Miss Moppet*. "Competitor number 16 is Best of Breed." She then swiveled around to face me, her overblown lips parting to display pearly whites gritted in a snarl. "And if I ever see *that* dog again, I'll personally neuter him."

And with that, she stomped her foot and strode out of the ring.

*****

Half an hour later, the hysterical yapping of small dogs and the ear-splitting crackle of an overhead PA system – background noises to complement the clash of crockery and low chatter in the showground's cafeteria – barely made a bump in my concentration as my fingers flew over the keyboard on my laptop.

After Busta had bombed out of his class, I'd returned my unrepentant canine to his crate, and decided to take myself off to a corner of the cafeteria, to be alone. As you do, when you consistently put out three steamy contemporary romance novels a year and your deadline for the third for the year was fast approaching. I also needed to work on Gray's personality. Transform him from a domineering out-for-what-he-could-get A-hole into a warm caring hero so Tabitha could fall in love with him.

Eyes glued to my computer screen, I typed faster…

Gray's probing tongue sent Tabitha's panties crackling as his kiss deepened. This was the night she'd been dreaming about for months. Her wedding night. The night she'd express her total unconditional love for her new husband, Ethan, Sydney's most eligible and wealthy bachelor, the man she'd planned to spend the rest of her life with. The man who'd left her at the altar, walked away from her, saying he wasn't ready for a marriage commitment, he was already overcommitted to running his three companies. But instead, here she was ready to hop into bed with the wrong man – for the wrong reasons. Gray, Ethan's best man at the wedding. Gray, who'd found her after her embarrassing rejection, hunched up behind a bush, crying, her wedding dress torn and dirty. He'd comforted her, taken her for a ride on the back of his Harley to the beach where she'd ended up in his arms.

But having sex with Gray, because she was angry with Ethan, was wrong on so many levels. Gray, a leather-clad biker with a conquest in every town, was only out for what he could get. Succumbing to his charms would only end in more heart-break. Or at the very least, a hot and steamy one-night stand with no meaning.

And that would make her feel cheap.

Resisting the inevitable pull his smoldering blue eyes, wild shoulder-length fair hair and strong tantalizing fingers were having on her libido, Tabitha pushed him away. "I'm sorry, Gray. I can't do this."

Gray's grip on her arms tightened. He yanked her closer. "Admit it. You want me!"

(No, no, he was still an A-hole… I chewed on one nail, deleted his words…replaced them.)

Gray instantly let her go and stepped back. "Are you sure, Tabitha?"

(Yes, that was better. Made Gray seem softer, more caring…)

Tabitha blinked up at him. "Think about it, Gray. You'd be cashing in on your best friend's wedding night, and I'd be getting back at him through you."

Eyes never leaving hers, he gently brushed a lock of hair from her face…

"Oof!" My chair clattered to the ground with a loud thump, as did my rear end, while my left elbow connected with an unyielding steel table leg.

"Oh dear, I'm so sorry. I wasn't looking where I was going."

The voice was deep, the plain brown shoes and cabbage green socks in my direct line of vision suggested male. A picture of Gray, with his aquiline nose, long shoulder length fair hair and sexy dimple drifted into my mind. Was this a re-enactment of a romantic 'cute meet' from one of my novels? Was this the man who would finally sweep me off my feet? If so, he'd certainly done a good job so far. I was sitting on the cafeteria floor.

Nursing my throbbing elbow, I peered up through a curtain of dark hair, and sighed. Nah. No romance hero here. It was only Harry Driscoll, a man in his late fifties. One of the many competitors who rocked up at a dog show week after week, hoping for a ribbon or trophy to take home.

Bottling my disappointment as merely a typical malfunction in my oh-so-predictable-and boring life, I gritted my teeth, ready to give the man leaning over me a piece of my mind. To tell him exactly what I thought of a guy who charged through a cafeteria like a bull in a china-shop, knocking inoffensive women off their chairs.

But something in the man's expression stopped me. Something that reminded me of a skinny ginger cat I'd found on death-row at an RSPCA facility two years ago when I'd been dropping off warm blankets for the animals. Panic? Fear? Dread? I'd taken the cat home with me, named him Flerken after Captain Marvel's feline friend, and he'd repaid my kindly act by shredding the sofa. *And* the lounge room curtains. *And* several important documents he took a dislike to on the kitchen table…

But Flerken was still around, still a little psycho, and spending most of his day on the desk in my office, either sleeping, destroying my papers, or stretched out across my keyboard preventing me from working.

"Here, let me help you up." The man sent a quick anxious glance over his shoulder before extending one hand and pulling me to my feet.

"Where's the fire?" I shook my head.

His returning smile, lips merely flattened, eyes everywhere but on me, said he didn't really get my poor joke.

"I'm sorry," he repeated, brushing what looked like dirt from the floor off my denim jacket. "Are you hurt?"

"I'll survive," I said. "But what about you? Harry, isn't it? I've seen you around the shows. Love your Giant Schnauzer, by the way. He's a real eye-catcher."

Harry's strained features softened momentarily and for the first time he actually looked at me. "Yes, Scout's as cute as a button. You should see him carrying his little toy ducky around the house. Such a gentle giant."

"You seem upset, Harry. Is there anything I can do to help?"

Harry's eyes connected with mine for a moment, as though he wanted to confide in me, and then he blinked, sent an anxious glance over his shoulder and his expression closed down. "No, no, I'm just running late to meet a-a…friend." He straightened his tie and sent another half-smile in my general direction. "Now, you have a good day."

And he was gone. Just like that.

I watched the man continue on through the cafeteria. He stumbled into another chair before reaching the door at the end and then disappeared through the opening.

Was he drunk? I hadn't picked up on the smell of alcohol, but I'd heard vodka was odorless. Maybe the poor guy had received bad news and drowned his sorrows in a bottle. And then I remembered the haunted look in his eyes. Was he in trouble? Was someone chasing him?

I straightened my chair and sat down again, tugging my laptop towards me ready to continue converting bad boy Gray into a realistic romance hero…but I'd lost the flow. The owner of the lovable Giant Schnauzer, had pushed both Gray and Tabitha's predicament out of my mind. Harry Driscoll was normally such a sweet little man. Who would he be running from?

"Aha! So, this is where you're hiding out. Heard on the grapevine that a certain evil fox terrier was kicked out of the showring for peeing on the judge's posh knee-high boots." My best friend, Abigail Truelove, grinning akin to the fictional Cheshire Cat, plonked herself down in the empty chair across from me and wiggled her eyebrows. "Now, that wouldn't be our saintly and oh-so-well-mannered *Sir Willowby of Cornwall*, would it?"

My other best friend, Dana Fox, her grin equally as large as Abi's, her hands overflowing with food – a sandwich, two chocolate biscuits and a jumbo-sized cream cake – carefully eased into the other empty chair and arranged her goodies on the table in front of her. While never putting on weight, Dana could eat her way through more food than both Abi and I put together. Probably needed the energy to keep up with her two over-active sprogs, both under four. If that was me, I'd need Valium to cope – not food. "And I also heard the poor judge had a fit of the vapors and had to go for a lie down." Dana shook her head in mock sorrow. "And to think Abi and I missed out on the entertainment because we were both competing for Best Hound in Group in another show ring. Unbelievable."

While Dana showed a stunning greyhound called Penelope, the gentlest dog in the universe, Abi's champion standard dachshund, Chloe, was also a regular contender for Best Hound in Group.

"Well, don't keep me in suspense. How'd you go?" I asked, purposely steering the discussion away from Busta's misdeeds.

"Judge barely gave us a second look. The Halliday's Afghan, *Butterwings Shillough,* performed like the star she is and swept all before her. And the judge gave runner-up to a basset hound." Dana tipped her head to one side and another grin wrinkled the corners of her lips. "But getting back to Busta's classy act today, did Lady Hamilton-Davies *really* threaten to neuter him if he ever came under her again?"

I decided the Busta story was getting old. Pretending I hadn't heard the question, I saved the latest *Three's A Crowd* document and shut down my laptop. Gray and Tabitha could stew in their own dramas for a while longer. Might sort themselves out and decide whether they wanted to get hot and personal. Or not. I wouldn't get any more work done with my friends here, and anyway, I was hungry. Trying to squeeze in some writing time before leaving for the dog show this morning, I'd ended up running too late to indulge in breakfast. It was now two in the afternoon. And that sandwich with the crisp lettuce, cheese, tomato, cucumber, avocado and what smelt like roast chicken sitting on the table in front of Dana looked tempting.

Then, without warning, Harry's frightened face popped into my head again. The more I thought about him, the more I believed he was running from someone when he knocked me over. I'd always thought of Harry as old-school. A gentleman. And to crash into me and then continue on with only a quick sorry, was not his style at all.

A chill came out of nowhere and scuttled in spiked boots up my spine. "Did either of you happen to see Harry Driscoll just before you entered the cafeteria?"

Abi frowned. "The guy with the Giant Schnauzer? No, but I did see him earlier in the day. He was talking to that oh-so-charming poodle breeder, Stephen Channing, over by the secretary's office." Abi's frown deepened. "Although, when I say, *talking,* I mean Stevie was being his usual bullying self, shouting at Harry and waving his arms, while poor Harry was huddled over, trying to shrink into a ball the size of a chocolate Jaffa. What Stevie's partner, Chi, sees in that man, I'll never know."

"Why do you want to know about Harry Driscoll?" asked Dana, biting into her cream cake with the delicacy of a mountain lion.

"It's probably nothing, but he blew through the cafeteria like a tornado on speed a few minutes before you arrived. Knocked me off my chair, sort of helped me to my feet, and then took off again. And by the expression on his face, plus his body language, I'd say the Monster from the Black Lagoon was after him with a well-sharpened pitchfork."

"Interesting." Abi had that glint in her eye. The one she gets when she smells a mystery. A month ago, she'd tripped over the dead body of the bimbo her ex-boyfriend was cheating on her with, which prompted the three of us to reinvent *The Gumshoe Chicks*, a sleuthing group formed way back in our high-school days, to solve the murder. I shivered. While Abi and Dana, my two gung-ho friends, relish taking on bad guys, me, I'm happy when I'm slap-bang in the world of my make-believe characters, channeling them into happy-ever-afters.

Getting involved with real life villains? Not so much.

Dana's tongue flicked out and she licked cream from the corner of her lips. When she spoke, her voice was matter-of-fact. "Did Harry say why he was in a hurry?"

"Something about running late to meet a friend."

Dana shrugged one shoulder as if the matter was closed. "Well, there you go. Mystery solved."

I screwed up my nose. Maybe Dana was right. Maybe I was dramatizing the whole affair. Still, Harry's behavior was odd and I couldn't get the image of his strained panicky face out of my head.

Chewing on a thumbnail which was already down to the quick, I felt around in my jacket pocket with the other hand. I was sure I'd dropped a packet of gum in there before I left home. Nothing helped settle my nerves like a packet of gum. And let's face it, gum tasted a hundred percent better than thumbnail. "Maybe you're right, Dana. But if he was meeting a friend – why did he look so terrified?"

"Might have had something to do with meeting a woman," put in Abi. "Perhaps Harry is having an affair?"

"In which case, Harry's love life is none of our business," said Dana.

"No, Harry's a gentleman. He's not like that. He wouldn't cheat on his wife."

"Molly, you are such a baby when it comes to relationships," said Abi, frowning. "I don't know how you manage to write all those steamy romance novels without learning something about the ways of men. You've barely said a dozen words to Harry Driscoll in the two years you've been showing Chloe. How would *you* know he's not like that?"

"Because he's a gentleman," I mumbled, my hand closing over the packet of gum in my pocket. "And gentlemen don't have affairs."

Abi gave a hoot while Dana chuckled into the last bite of her cream cake. She wiped her lips with the back of her hand and reached for her sandwich. Food was rarely eaten in regular order when Dana was hungry. What with a full-time job running her own mobile dog wash, *Hydro Hound*, plus two gorgeous but demanding kids and a husband who adored her, Dana had learned to grab food whenever a small block of time opened for her. The order of eating that food was the last of her concerns. "Did he say anything specific to make you think he was in trouble?"

Along with the gum, a crumpled piece of paper that hadn't been in my pocket before I entered the cafeteria, tumbled out.

"Where did that come from?" I said, attempting to flatten the paper out on the table. "It's not mine."

And then I remembered Harry brushing non-existent dust from my jacket after he'd helped me from the floor.

"It was Harry. He must have slipped this into my pocket while brushing me down."

We all stared at the three words scrawled in black text across the paper. The words that sent my heart into orbit and Abi and Dana's eyebrows somewhere up around their hairline.

YOU'RE DEAD HARRY.

"Right." Abi's chair made a scratching sound on the wooden floor as she bounced to her feet. "Looks like we have another mystery to solve."

"Hang on," said Dana, the voice of reason. "Why should *we* get involved? It's not like Harry Driscoll is our best friend. We only know him enough to say hello and nod our head when we pass him at a dog show."

"What? So, we're going to sit back, knowing Harry's been threatened, and do nothing about it?"

"Nooo." Dana rolled her eyes. "But we're only going to *find* Harry. Advise him to go to the police. Ask him if he knows who sent the note. That's all." She reached for the other half of her sandwich before hefting her family-sized bag over her shoulder. "'Cos you *do* realize this is a death threat? And that means there's a wannabe murderer out there who wrote it?"

A wannabe murderer…

I sat staring down at the three words on the crumpled sheet of paper. I knew 'terrified' when I saw it and Harry had been radiating all the signs.

And no wonder…

But did I really want to find out who sent that note?

2

Seemed like news of Busta's party trick had spread around the dog show like a bottle of molasses dropped on a cement floor. A group of Bedlington-terrier owners sniggered and pointed as I sidled past their camp site. Not the first to react since we'd left the relative privacy of the cafeteria and gone looking for Harry.

"Let's start with Stephen Channing," suggested Dana, leading the way over to a large rainbow-colored bus with *Windswept Kennels* painted in decorative letters on the side. "See if he knows where Harry is."

"And maybe find out what caused the big argument earlier today," put in Abi, sending a stink-eye glare in the direction of the still-chuckling Bedlington-terrier owners for my benefit. Without Abi and Dana's protection and friendship during high school, I wouldn't have survived the bullying. And even today, they still watched out for me.

Set up next to their rainbow-hued bus, Stephen and his partner, Chi, were busy preparing one of their poodles for its next class. Well, Chi was busy brushing, fluffing and spraying, while Stephen was more into adding ear rings and a chunky gold bangle to his already ostentatious show ring attire.

The moment Stephen caught sight of me, his eyes lit up, his body language shouted let's-make-fun-of-gullible-Molly, and he let loose a loud braying guffaw. "How long did it take to teach your fleabag that trick?" he called out, his voice carrying to the other side of the showgrounds. "And what's he going to do for an encore? Drop a brick?"

Heat warming my face, I stared down at my shoes, while the man dressed like he was booked to perform a vaudeville act on the stage instead of showing his dog in the ring, continued to laugh in that sneeringly hateful way that made my skin crawl.

Why couldn't I be more forceful, like Dana and Abi? Tell the bully exactly where he could go and what he could do when he got there?

I needed to grow a backbone. Stop being so worried about what other people thought of me. Thanks to my Great-Granny Teresa's archaic upbringing, where children were seen and not heard and the words and definitions of *sex* and *love*, and all their varied connotations, were inked out of every Dictionary in the household, courtesy of a permanent marker, I was not only naive emotionally – still a virgin at 27 – but also crushingly insecure. I often wondered what my life might have been like if my parents hadn't died in a horror car crash when I was four.

But hey, I wasn't four any more…

"You're not really funny, you know, Stephen." I flashed him a facsimile of my scary face, the one I sometimes practiced in my bedroom mirror. "Try pathetic."

Dana raised one eyebrow and sent me an approving grin, before turning back to the now-scowling poodle breeder. "Have you seen Harry Driscoll in the last half hour, Stephen?"

"Why would I be looking for *that* nobody?"

"Because you were seen arguing with *that* nobody earlier today and now he's missing. What was the argument about?" Abi's fierce stink-eye never wavered from Stephen's face.

"Who told you that rubbish?"

Dana sighed. "Stephen, you were heard shouting at the man, so don't deny it. Now, what were you arguing about?"

Chi, Stephen's finely-boned Asian boyfriend, a sweet guy who could bake a really mean cookie, looked up from his task of grooming their stunning apricot standard poodle, *Supreme Champion, Windswept Fly By Me* and shook his head. "It was nothing, Dana." His voice was soft and sing-song. "Stevie became a little upset when Harry let his Giant Schnauzer off the leash and the big dog scared one of our babies. This happened moments before she was due to go in the show ring and it spoilt her chances of winning. Made her nervous and she didn't show well."

"That blasted dog's a menace," snarled Stevie, the four gold chains displayed on his bare chest where he'd undone the top buttons of his blue satin shirt clanking together and emphasizing his words. "And so is his owner. Keeps telling everyone how sweet and gentle his darling Scout is – and he's not. Blasted dog doesn't know its own strength. Went to play with little Heidi and knocked her flat, left her screaming. Couldn't calm her down and she bombed out in her class." His scowl deepened. "And the stupid little man blamed Heidi. Said she was a drama queen and that Scout was traumatized because Heidi didn't want to be his friend." He shook his head. "That man needs someone to knock some sense into him."

Buoyed by my growing confidence, I took a step closer. "And is that what you told him, Stephen? That after the show you'd get him in a quiet corner and teach him some manners?"

Stephen's frown deepened further until his eyebrows almost touched his nose. "Hey, I don't know what your interest in Harry Driscoll is, but I didn't threaten him, and I don't know where he is. Now, I'm busy, I have a dog waiting for me to exhibit, and I don't have to answer your questions. If you want to find Harry, go look for him elsewhere." A loose-lipped smirk twisted the poodle-breeder's face. "Maybe check out Rhianna Hamilton-Davies, the judge whose boots your dog mistook for a fire hydrant. Harry's always making goo-goo eyes at her – and every other woman on the circuit." He grimaced. "Although, if you've seen that lump of play-dough he calls his wife, you'll understand *why* he looks elsewhere. Whatever. But, he's not here."

And with that, Stephen turned his back on us and flounced across to

Chi.

A little taken-aback, I raised an eyebrow at Dana and Abi. "Harry's playing around with Lady Hamilton-Davies, the show judge? But Harry's a gentleman. And-and she's married to the Mayor."

"Don't believe everything that comes out of Stephen's mouth," warned Dana. "One – his filter's clogged with the sludge of his own ego. And two – he gets great pleasure from stirring the pot and creating scandal where there's none."

"So, what next?" said Abi.

"We keep looking for Harry," said Dana, taking control and striding ahead. "First up, we find their camp and talk to his wife. Who knows? Harry might even be there now, preparing his dog for the show-ring."

After questioning a nearby Schnauzer competitor, without success, we came across a large white van with *McInerny's Schnauzer Kennels* emblazoned in large letters on the sides. Beside the van, two noisy mini Schnauzers, four standards and a large handsome giant regarded us from inside their individual dog crates.

Other than the dogs, there didn't seem to be anyone else around.

"Hellooo!" Dana called out. "Anyone here?"

A man, mid to late fifties, hair prematurely gray, slid open the side door of the white van and stepped out onto the grass. He was attempting to shove both arms into the sleeves of a brightly colored Hawaiian shirt but in his haste kept missing the left sleeve hole.

"Any idea where Harry Driscoll is?" Dana asked, while Abi and I bent down to exchange baby talk with the two bouncing minis through the bars of their individual crates. They acted like squirming toddlers begging to be picked up.

The man, Mr. McInerny I suppose, as he'd exited the McInerny van, hastily finished donning his shirt and after fastening the last button, regarded us with a loud sniff. "No idea, but I think I saw the Driscolls set up camp somewhere over there." With a lift of his head, he indicated a quiet spot in amongst several trees and bushes on the outskirts of the dog arenas. "He and his wife usually like to get away from the crowds."

The Driscoll camp was exactly where Mr. McInerny had indicated. Harry's dog, Scout, was curled up asleep in what had to be the largest crate on the market, while Mrs. Driscoll relaxed in one of the two folding canvas chairs set under the shade of a century-old ghost gum. Large pink headphones covered both her ears. While bopping to music only she could hear, she was knitting what looked to be a baby's shawl – for their newest grand-child, due next month, she told us as she pulled off her ear phones and greeted us with a welcoming smile and an invitation to call her Lizzie.

Lizzie Driscoll was no oil painting, but Stephen Channing's' snide words, 'lump of play-dough he calls a wife', were overly cruel. Okay, she was overweight, her eyes too close together and her mouth too large, but her face radiated inner kindness. It was the face of a woman who'd served many years caring unconditionally for her family. And not herself. A controlled diet, an inventive hairdresser, some choice cosmetics and spending money on well-fitting clothes instead of grabbing the nearest size 22 off the rack, would see Lizzie Driscoll metamorphize into, maybe not a breathtakingly beautiful butterfly, but a very pretty member of the moth family.

I smiled down at her. "Hi, Mrs. Driscoll. We're looking for Harry. Is he around?"

"No, dear. I haven't seen him since he went off to the Gents about three-quarters of an hour ago. Must have got caught up gossiping with one of his mates." She shook her head. "If he doesn't get back soon though, I'll have to ask someone to give him a call over the loudspeaker. Scout's class is due to start in about ten minutes and I can't manage the dog myself." She flexed her dimpled left leg cautiously. "Crook knee, you know. Been waiting a year now for a knee replacement. The Health System's a shamble under this present government. You know, my next-door-neighbor, Dora, she's been waiting almost three years for a–
"

"Does Harry normally leave it this late to prepare his dog for the ring?" Dana cut in before Lizzie could embark on Dora's entire health history.

"No, not really." She blinked like a startled owl as though the seriousness of her predicament was only now hitting home. "In fact, Harry's what you might call, a stickler for detail. Always has Scout brushed, polished, warmed up and waiting at the entry gate, well before his class is due to start." Her knitting dropped to her lap, forgotten, as she started chewing nervously on the head of one of the large green plastic knitting needles. "Maybe I'd better get that call over the loudspeaker now."

This didn't seem like a typical Harry thing to do – leave his wife to show Scout without warning. I took a step closer, smile still in place. We didn't want to alarm her. "Did Harry seem anxious, or worried when he left? You know, to go to the Gents?"

"Um…well, he did seem a little edgy. Usually goes over and reassures Scout before he leaves, tells him Daddy won't be long. But he didn't this time." She frowned in thought. "He took a phone call, didn't say who it was, and then rushed off as though a pack of wolves were after him. I just thought he'd been cut short – you know – and needed to get to the Gents in a hurry." She looked around as if expecting her errant husband to materialize out of the blue, then shook her head. "This is not like Harry at all, you know. What will I do if he's not back in time for Scout's class?"

Dana shrugged one shoulder. "Would you like me to take Scout in the ring for you? I show a greyhound, so I'm accustomed to large dogs."

"Oh, would you, dear? That's very kind of you. Scout's collar and lead are hanging on a hook on the side of his crate and you'll find his grooming gear all laid out neat and tidy inside a brown leather box behind the crate." She reached down for a walking stick lying on the ground beside her. "While you get Scout out and groom him, I'll go fetch his little yellow ducky from the trailer. Playing with his favorite toy always brightens him up before he goes into the ring. It makes him show better."

I placed a hand on her shoulder. "You stay where you are, Lizzie. If you just tell me where Scout's yellow ducky is, I'll go fetch it then when I get back Dana and I can get Scout brushed and shiny and warmed up for his class." I could see she was having trouble getting up off the canvas chair, even with the help of a walking stick and hoped the Health System didn't leave her waiting for that knee-replacement too much longer.

"Thank you, dear." Lizzie smiled up at me with that too large mouth that merely enhanced the sweetness of her smile. "His ducky is inside the front berth of our dog trailer. The toy's a bit beat up now but he still loves it." She pointed to a white car and matching trailer parked about 50 meters away, behind a row of scraggly bottlebrush bushes that looked like they hadn't seen pruning shears since Ned Kelly was a boy. "We always park away from the others. Makes it easier to pack up and leave when the show's over."

While Dana hooked the big black and white dog up with his collar and lead, I climbed the hill to the dog trailer. The area here, at the back of the show-grounds was so peaceful. I could hear doves cooing to each other over by the fence line and the honeyed smell of the bottlebrush wafted across my path.

The Driscoll's dog trailer was larger than the average trailer. Probably because Scout was larger than the average dog. And judging by the life-like painting of their beloved black shiny dog on both sides, he was now being lavished with all the love and affection recently given to their grown-up kids, who'd packed up and left the nest.

As I moved closer, I could see the door to the front berth was slightly ajar. Had Harry forgotten to close it? Or had vandals been messing around with the trailer? It was hidden by the bottlebrush, a distance from their camp, and Lizzie's headphones would mean kids could have been playing nearby without being heard.

Hoping there was no major damage, I pushed my way between two bottlebrush bushes, reached for the door handle…and stopped.

The sun seemed to disappear behind a cloud. A chilly breeze whipped up out of nowhere. The birds stopped cooing and flew away.

There, poking out of the partly open door of the trailer, was a brown shoe. A man's brown shoe. In fact, it looked exactly like the shoes Harry was wearing when I sprawled beside him on the floor of the cafeteria. I blinked. Swallowed the sudden lump in my throat. Even down to the same cabbage green socks.

Was Harry asleep inside the dog trailer? Or hiding from whoever was threatening him?

Hand shaking, breath a rusty chainsaw in my throat, I tentatively used one finger to nudge the trailer door open wider and look inside.

Harry was curled up in a fetal ball, his knees almost touching his chin. But he wasn't hiding. And he wasn't asleep. His eyes, wide open, were unseeing. And there was a pair of long-bladed grooming scissors embedded deep in his chest.

3

A black car, the paintwork glinting in the afternoon sunlight, rolled imperiously across the showgrounds. It cruised past uniformed police stringing up yellow and black crime-scene tape, curious wide-eyed dog owners, and three paramedics who'd earlier declared Harry Driscoll dead at the scene of the crime. The black car, its engine purring almost silently, came to a smooth stop no more than six feet away from us. Immediately, a uniformed constable, his tongue lolling like a dog eager to please his master, broke away from interviewing bystanders and hurried across to the car. He opened the door for the driver, a straight-shouldered man in a dark blue suit, and stepped back, waiting for the man to exit the vehicle.

Aquiline nose inclined upward, Detective Lightfoot glanced around the crime scene, spoke to the constable who was now closing the car door behind him and then, authority in every movement, strode toward us. His icy blue orbs already zeroing in on Abi, Dana and me.

I blew out a breath of air I'd unconsciously been holding while watching the progress of the car across the showgrounds. The man in charge had officially arrived.

"I'm Detective Lightfoot," he said flashing a warrant card at us, his expression that of someone who'd unavoidably stepped in a steaming pile of cow dung.

As usual…not happy to see us.

"Good afternoon, Detective," said Abi, with a slight lift of one eyebrow. We'd all clashed with this detective before, but Abi had more reason to be on her toes. The man had already falsely accused her of one murder in the past.

"Which one of you ladies found the body?" His words were clipped, and his eyes narrowed as he glared at us. Almost like he thought we enjoyed tripping over dead bodies and calling him away from his afternoon tea to investigate.

"I did." I had to force the words through parched lips. "I found Harry when I went to get Scout's yellow ducky from the trailer."

"Scout? Who's Scout?"

"The Driscoll's Giant Schnauzer."

He shrugged one shoulder. "And why would you do that?"

"Harry was late for his class, so Dana offered to show the dog for Lizzie…Harry's wife. She couldn't show him because of her knee….and I offered to get the dog's toy out of the trailer." When the detective looked blank, I added, "It gets him on his toes and makes him show better."

I turned away to dig into Lizzie's picnic bag, found a bottle of water and handed it to her. The poor woman was having trouble breathing. She was hunched over on her canvas chair while two constables lobbed questions at her like darts at a dart board. Her white knitting, now speckled with dirt, lay between her feet on the ground.

Anyone with half a brain and a modicum of compassion could see Lizzie was incapable of answering their questions – her husband had been brutally murdered. Instead of harassing her, the police should contact Lizzie's family so they could take her home and care for her.

"What did you do when you opened the trailer door?"

Dragging myself reluctantly back into the firing line, I blinked up at the detective's steely eyes and granite jaw. I shook my head at him. "What does anyone do when they find a dead body? I lost it." To show him what I meant, I lifted my stained shirt in his direction, then quickly turned my head away as the smell of vomit infiltrated my nostrils. I didn't think the detective actually wanted a visual demonstration in answer to his question.

"And did you touch the deceased?"

Deceased? I cringed. Felt the last dregs of my thermos coffee threatening to make an appearance. "O-only to feel for a pulse."

I hadn't wanted to touch him. I'd even squeezed my eyes closed as I leaned forward, blindly reaching for the pulse point on Harry's left wrist. But quickly opened them again when my hand brushed against the bloody scissors.

I shivered, goosebumps competing with the raised hairs all along both arms. "But there was no pulse. Nothing. He-he was dead."

"And the murder weapon?" Lightfoot's voice continued on, steely, relentless, as though I wasn't shaking and in danger of once-again losing control of my stomach contents. "Did you recognize the murder weapon?"

"What do you mean?" His words, like a bucket of ice water, jolted me out of my malaise. "Why would I recognize the murder weapon? All I had time to make out before covering my shirt and sneakers with puke was a pair of blood-splattered scissors. And no, I didn't stop to examine them to see if the murderer's initials were engraved on the handles."

Lightfoot cocked one eyebrow. "Several show competitors already interviewed by my men have recognized the murder weapon as a pair of professional dog grooming scissors used to trim dogs' legs and beards. Toledo steel and strong and pointy." His eyes bore into mine. "So, my next question is – are they yours?"

There hadn't been time for me to fully fall apart yet – I'd do that later in the privacy of my bedroom – but if I didn't get away from this insensitive detective questioning me as though I was capable of ramming a pair of scissors deep into a man's heart, I'd end up screaming until the detective's ears disintegrated.

"Hey, watch what you're saying!" Like a little cock sparrow, Abi stepped right up into the detective's space. "Or you'll have a defamation charge filed against you. Molly exhibits a smooth fox terrier in the show ring. The operative word being, *smooth*. In fact, there's not a hair on Busta long enough to trim with scissors. So, if you're looking for the owner of those deadly babies protruding from Harry Driscoll's chest, go do some real police-work and investigate the competitors who show *long-haired* breeds."

The stone-faced suit's eyes never left mine. It was as though he couldn't, or wouldn't listen to Abi's explanation.

"You haven't answered my question, Ms. Gibson. Are the dog grooming scissors yours?"

I shook my head. If I opened my mouth, I might say something that could leave me in handcuffs.

"And what did you think when you saw Harry's body in the trailer?"

"Wh-what did I think?" I could hear the crack in my voice. The growing sense of losing control. "Well, Detective Lightfoot, the only dead body I've seen before today was that of a squashed cat on the road outside my unit. A cat that had been run over by so many buses trucks and cars it was merely bits of bloody flesh and fur on the bitumen. So, the fact that I immediately transferred my breakfast of snap, crackle and pop from my stomach into the gutter, and the poor squashed cat invaded my dreams for weeks after the nice man from the Council came to remove it, that was mere peanuts compared to how I felt after finding Harry." I took a choking breath through a throat that had clogged with tears. "So no, I didn't feel too good after opening the trailer door and seeing, not a little yellow ducky as I'd expected, but Harry's dead body."

"Right, that's it!" said Dana, slipping one arm through mine while Abi captured my other arm. "If you want to ask my friend any more questions you know where she lives. We're taking Molly home now. She's had a terrible shock and you, with your totally insensitive questions, are not helping."

"Sir! Sir! We've found something, sir!" The same eager-beaver constable with the lolling tongue galloped toward us, all waving arms and overt enthusiasm. He held the Driscoll's leather grooming bag in the air like an Olympic trophy. "It's not in here, sir. The Driscoll's grooming scissors. The space where they're supposed to be is labelled but the scissors are missing. We believe they're the same scissors used to murder the victim."

"Good work, Constable Graham. Escort Mrs. Driscoll back to the police station, read her her rights and I'll question her further once I arrive."

And with that, the stony-faced detective slid back into his shiny black car, moved his rear vision mirror a miniscule to the left and drove off.

Lizzie the murderer? I watched in shock as the constable, all fired up on his boss's praise, swaggered over to Harry's wife, said something to her and then produced a set of handcuffs from his back pocket which he fastened around her wrists.

"No, no, not Lizzie." I pulled away from Dana and Abi and raced across to the shaking, distraught woman. "Mrs. Driscoll loved her husband. No way would she kill him."

"You've got the wrong person, Constable," said Abi, close on my heels. "Anyone could have taken those scissors from the Driscoll's grooming box. There's a couple hundred people competing at the show today."

"Someone framed you, Lizzie." Dana pushed past the constable to get closer to the trembling, pale-faced woman. "Think, Lizzie. Is there anyone who hated your husband? Anyone he's crossed in the past?"

"No, everyone loved my Harry." Lizzie swayed on her feet.

"Come on, think, Lizzie," persisted Dana. "Was he involved with a criminal element? Did he tread on someone's toes so badly they wanted revenge?"

"I'll have to insist you stop talking to our suspect," growled Constable Up-Himself, frowning as he planted himself bodily between Lizzie and us. "Or I'll charge you with obstruction."

As two policemen almost carried the distraught Lizzie towards a police cruiser, Abi called out, "Don't worry about Scout, I'll look after him until someone from your family comes to pick him up."

Typical Abi. Always rescuing animals.

Of course, Dana had to sweeten the pot further. "Keep your chin up, Lizzie," she called out. "You'll be out of jail before you can say, 'slip stitch, knit purl. 'Cos we'll make it our personal business to find out who killed your Harry."

I let out a shaky sigh.

Seemed like the *Gumshoe Chicks* were back on the trail again…

*****

I wrapped both my hands around the glass of Riesling Abi handed me – my third for the night – and took a large satisfying gulp, the sweet fruitiness of the white wine stimulating my palate. Okay, I knew I was close to my limit but all I wanted to do was blot out the sight of Harry's waxy dead face, even if it meant drinking myself into oblivion.

And if that resulted in me sleeping on Abi's couch tonight and waking with sledgehammers and fireworks competing for primacy inside my skull in the morning – that was preferable to reliving over and over in my dreams, the sickening moment I'd peered into the Driscoll's trailer at the showgrounds.

'Cos after three glasses of alcohol I'd have no dreams….

After the police marched Lizzie off to jail, we'd packed up and driven straight to Abby's house. Our place of refuge. I vaguely remembered hearing Dana on the phone to her husband, Peter, explaining why she wouldn't be home until later and to make sure Jake had his cough medicine before bed and not to read any scary stories to their three-year-old, Kayla. Evidently the last time Peter had been allocated bedtime-story duties, he'd read them the next chapter of his current Steven King novel.

"What I don't understand," said Abby sharing a blanket with Chloe, her smoochy smooth dachshund who'd climbed up onto her lap, "is how anyone could get a dead body past a hundred show competitors and into that trailer without being seen?"

Dana shook her head. "I'm betting Harry met his killer at the trailer and he was murdered there."

"But why didn't his wife see or hear him?"

"She was listening to music on her headphones and her eyes were on her knitting."

"Poor Harry," I said and hiccupped loudly.

"Think that better be your last glass of wine, Molly. You're going to be a mess tomorrow."

"Tomorrow?" said Dana rolling her eyes. "She's a mess now."

I sniffed. "Do you blame me?"

"I just remembered," said Abi. "Did you give that piece of paper with the death threat Harry slipped into your pocket to the police?"

I hiccupped again, put my glass down on the coffee table between us chairs, and shook my head. Which was the wrong thing to do as the floor and ceiling suddenly changed places. Very disconcerting. "No. I don't trust that detective guy."

I'd witnessed my first human dead body, the front of my shirt and my sneakers were covered in vomit and all I wanted was to do was get as far away from the scene of the crime as I could, but Detective Lightfoot had rubbed me up the wrong way.

Especially when he'd zeroed in on me because I'd found the body, and then on some flimsy evidence, turned his flawed logic on Lizzie Driscoll and accused her of her husband's murder. What time during that insanity was there to think rationally?

"Well, where is it now?" asked Dana.

"Still in my jacket pocket."

And as my jacket was hanging on the back of Abi's bedroom door, an exhausting twenty yards away from where I was draped across the sofa, I decided it could stay there. The rest of my smelly clothes, washed and put through the drier were now airing out on a wooden clothes horse in Abi's passageway. All now smelling of lilac instead of vomitus. A hot shower, followed by a riffle through Abi's wardrobe saw me now dressed in her blue jeans and a black tee shirt proclaiming me as 'Witch of the Year'.

"Stay there, I'll go get it." Abi carefully moved Chloe off her lap and stood up, almost stumbling over Harry's dog, Scout, who'd made himself at home on the fluffy black and white woolen rug at her feet. Penelope, Dana's greyhound, was roached beside the newcomer, four legs in the air, while Busta had his nose buried deep inside the large red plastic toy box in the corner of the room, probably hunting for 'just the right toy' to entice his canine friends into playing a game with him.

"This is a major clue," Abi proclaimed returning with the screwed-up death threat. She flattened the paper out on the coffee table and we all leaned forward to re-read the chilling words, YOU'RE DEAD HARRY.

I picked up the note by the top corners, brought it within two inches of my face and squinted, checked every minuscule speck of the paper – and that's when I saw it. Okay, maybe it was due to the note being right under my nose, or maybe the Gods of Wine were looking over my shoulder – but when I studied the paper more closely, I could just make out the word *Boop* printed in cartoony text on the edge, where the paper had been torn off a larger sheet.

"Hey, look at this!"

Dana leaned closer. "Look at what? Where?"

"Here, where it says, *Boop*."

"Boop?" repeated Dana, screwing up her nose. "What sort of word is that?"

"Well, the only thing I can associate *Boop* with is the cartoon character *Betty Boop*." I wriggled my eyebrows at them and grinned. "I'd say that paper's been ripped from a *Betty Boop* writing pad."

"Hey, good pick up, Moll," said Abi returning my grin as she took the paper to check it out.

"We'll make a detective of you yet," added Dana.

Resisting the urge to puff out my chest, I gave them both a thumbs-up.

"But you still need to get this to the police," Dana continued, bringing me down to earth again with a bump. "Maybe they employ a Forensic handwriting expert who can trace the sender."

"Duh. We know who sent it. The murderer, " I said, stating the obvious as I attempted to place my half-full glass back on the coffee table, couldn't seem to find the table, and promptly decided it was safer to finish off the wine first. "The murderer threatened to kill Harry and then went ahead and did it."

Abi let out a sigh. "Yeah, but who? And why?"

"That's the million-dollar question," said Dana. "The Harry Driscoll we knew seemed such an inoffensive old softie. Unless he was a covert drug dealer, or a clandestine womanizer, I can't for the life of me work out why anyone would want him dead."

"And as for suspects," added Abi shaking her head. "Any one of the competitors at the show today could have taken those scissors from the Driscoll's grooming box. They only had to wait until Lizzie went to buy a coffee or to the Rest Room or..."

"And what about her headphones?" I added, remembering how sweet Lizzie looked bopping to her music when we found her. "With those on, she wouldn't have heard if a mob of wild brumbies galloped past."

"The police always suspect the spouse in these cases," said Dana twisting a lock of her chestnut-colored hair around one finger. "Let's hope when forensics check the murder weapon it's not the scissors that went missing from the Driscoll's grooming box."

"Lizzie Driscoll loved her husband," I wailed. Yep...wailed. I'd drained my third glass of wine and was now licking the dregs from the rim of the glass. "She's not a murderer."

"Well, let's hope Stephen Channing was way off-beam when he accused Harry of being involved with other women. But if he's right and Lizzie found out about her husband's indiscretions, that would give her a first-class motive."

Abi leaned forward on her chair, eyes alight with anticipation. "Or," she drew the word out, rolled it around in her mouth like a much-loved candy. "What if Harry rejected the Mayor's wife. Told her he wanted to break it off?"

"And they had a fight," added Dana, eyes lighting up.

"And she had a pair of grooming scissors in her pocket at the time and in a fit of rage stabbed him with them?"

"Yeees!" I broke in. Happy to accuse the snippy show judge of murder and let Lizzie off the hook.

"Or what if her husband found out Harry was having an affair with his wife and killed him?"

"Exactly," said Dana. "So, let's go have a chat with Rhianna Hamilton-Davies tomorrow. See what we can find out."

Rhianna Hamilton-Davies… the judge whose boots Busta ruined?

Knowing I would later regret the action, I made a wild grab for Abi's untouched glass of wine parked on the coffee table between us. Leaning my head back, I closed my eyes and let the wine slide down my throat.

My fourth for the night – a new record.

But if I had to confront that snippy show judge again, I'd not only need my check-book, I'd need all the backbone I could drink.

4

When I pulled up outside my own abode around nine Monday morning – I'd spent all of Sunday at Abi's – Flerken, my opinionated ginger tabby cat was waiting for me. And he was far from happy.

The moment I stumbled through the front door of my unit, he stalked from the kitchen, tail high and quivering, expression that of a very ticked off spouse demanding an explanation for this unsolicited sojourn.

Thoroughly peeved, the cat let out a loud and ear-piercing yowl that set the forest of jangling bells inhabiting my brain into cacophonous chaos. Also re-awakened the fiendish little hammer-wielding goblins who'd been quietly reheating their instruments of torture, just waiting for a reason to reappear. Actively and noisily.

"Flerken, please, be quiet." Lifting a shaky finger, I pointed to his automatic waterer and equally automatic kibble dispenser. "You can't be hungry. And I don't need your permission to stay at my friend's house overnight. Right?"

He evidently disagreed with both statements. His frown grew so deep all I could see of his eyes were two dark pupils which were fast becoming narrow slits. He tossed his head, gave an even louder yowl, and then stalked ahead of me into the kitchen, where he sat like a stone in front of a white cupboard with marble-gray trim. A cupboard stacked with his gourmet tins of mackerel & salmon, grilled chicken and rice, ocean whitefish tuna, and those little silver sardines he swallows without chewing.

Busta, who'd trailed through the doorway behind me, spotted Flerken's twitching tail as the cat made his grand departure toward the kitchen, and decided to follow. Once there, he gently nosed Flerken, *hello*, then plopped his rear end on the polished wooden floor beside him. If Flerken was going to be fed, then this was definitely the place to be. After all, the white and gray cupboard also contained Busta's favorite gourmet meals. Grilled chicken, lean farm-reared beef, and lamb & kangaroo stew.

Then, while the torturers in my head performed a Mediaeval war dance, accompanied by clashing cymbals and the *boom-boom* of multiple kettle drums, I fiddled blindly around in the cupboard drawers until my fingers fastened around the tin opener. *Thank you, God*. Now, if I could just stop my head from exploding and splattering tissue and brains all over the kitchen walls until I fed my two furry dictators, I'd then be able to medicate, drink a gallon of water and crash in peace.

Several hours later, it was the persistently loud banging on my front door that woke me…

Opening one bleary eye, I checked the time on my bedside clock. 12.30. I took that as in the afternoon and not the following morning, as I'd planned to meet up with the other two *Gumshoe Chicks* at Abi's boutique, *Pampered Pooch*, at 2.00p.m.

We were going to confront the lioness – Rhianna Hamilton-Davies – in her den. My excuse, a check to pay for the damage done by my naughty canine. Our real reason, to ask questions about her involvement with Harry.

I dragged myself off the bed, where I'd collapsed after climbing the stairs three-and-a-half hours ago, and ran a hand through stiff, bed-tousled hair. I took a wary peek in the mirror on the wardrobe door and let out a shriek. *That couldn't be me!* Still dressed in Abi's too-big jeans and black tee from the night before, my normally shiny long black hair looked like it had been plugged into an electric socket. Or put through a wind-tunnel. And the anemic face staring back at me could easily have belonged to the Bad Witch of the North.

I was already wearing the tee-shirt. All I needed was a tall pointy hat and a straw broom…

The banging on my front door started up again, louder this time, together with Busta's high pitched bark, which told me the door-knocker was a stranger.

Was Harry's murderer out there? A bloody pair of scissors in one hand and an axe in the other, just waiting for me to open the door before plunging both into my skinny neck?

Or had the police decided to release Lizzie and arrest me instead?

For goodness sake, Molly Gibson, pull yourself together and act like a grown up. It was my Great-Granny Teresa's voice. With very little effort she'd squashed the fire-toting goblins, silenced the cacophonous bells, and hijacked my head.

These were words I'd heard many times during my childhood and I'd learned at a young age how to react to them. Stifle the quiver in my bottom lip, swallow my fear and walk tall. Even if my hair was a fright, my face could grace the cover of a paranormal novel and my clothes were definitely of the slept-in variety.

'Coming!" I shouted, stomping down the stairs, while attempting to pat my hair into submission. "No need to bang the door down."

Flerken immediately scooted out from the kitchen to arch and rub up against my legs, his plaintive meow and wide 'I'm feeling unloved' eyes demanding to be picked up and cuddled. I shook my head at him, telling him 'later'. Then, with Busta dancing around my ankles, yapping, bouncing, threatening death by a thousand licks to the intruder, I cracked the front door open to the end of the security chain and peered out.

Hmm… Even in a black leather biker jacket and heavy motor bike boots, the guy standing on my doorstep didn't *look* like a murderer. And he didn't appear to be a policeman either. In fact, he reminded me of Gray, the hunky hero, the third wheel in the love-triangle romance I was currently writing. Thick wavy fair hair spread across his shoulders, body that itched to be explored, and lips that were so kissable, so moreish, when I went to speak, I found my tongue stuck to the roof of my mouth.

"What-what-who-who are you?" I finally got out.

Oh great, Molly Gibson, that's really intelligent. I sighed. Great Granny Teresa at work again.

"I'm Hudson Driscoll, Harry's son. Open the door!"

Harry's son? I hesitated. Frowned. Okay, his lips might be kissable, but at the moment they appeared ready to open wide, produce a set of sharp teeth and rip my head off. His hair was almost as wild as mine and his eyes, bluer than the sea, were threatening to drown me.

While Busta continued to bounce up and down, scratching at the door, I scowled at the stranger through the two-inch opening. "How do I know you're who you say you are? For all I know, you could have a pair of grooming scissors stashed in your pocket. You could be Harry's murderer."

He returned my scowl with a sneering touch of derision. "Do I look like a murderer?"

I eyed him up and down, slowly, quite enjoying the ride. "I don't know what a murderer looks like, do I?"

Was that his teeth I could hear grinding together? Or was it growling noises deep in his throat? Finally, he inhaled a deep breath before letting it out slowly as though forcing himself to calm down. He put both hands in the pockets of his black leather jacket and came out empty. "See, no scissors. Now let me in. I need to talk to you."

"Still not happening."

"For God's…"

"What do you want to talk about?"

"You found my Dad…"

"Yes, and I'm sorry for your loss. I didn't know your father very well but he seemed like a nice man. A man who didn't deserve to die like that."

It was as though I'd pricked him with a sharp needle as I watched him deflate in front of me. He rubbed at his eyes with the back of his hand and took a deep steadying breath. He was either distressed by his father's death, or an Academy Award actor. "Please, let me in. I want to know what happened. Although my mother's been released from custody for the moment, she's still in shock." He shook his head, his blue eyes steady. "All I want to do is talk."

Heart in mouth, I unhooked the chain and opened the door, then stepped back, my eyes searching the room for a likely weapon. Busta, my so-called guard dog, had up and deserted me, too busy untying the guy's shoe laces and wagging his tail. As for Flerken, he'd stalked off back to the kitchen, in a right royal huff. So, if Harry's son grew angry again, I was on my own.

There was a cheesy-looking $10.99 lamp I'd bought at the last Black Friday sales squatting on the table nearby. The base was heavy enough to crack a skull open if necessary, but after weighing up the pros and cons, I decided against it as a weapon. Geez, I already looked like a bad imitation of a fairy-tale witch, so just how ridiculous would I look toting a lamp under my arm while attempting to find out whether this guy was Harry's son or his murderer? Instead, I picked up a lead doorstopper in the shape of a fox terrier. Still heavy, but easier to maneuver and just as deadly when applied with force to the back of a person's skull.

"Come into the kitchen," I said, remembering that's where I'd left my cell phone while feeding my two fur-babies earlier. If I could put the police on speed dial while distracting Hudson with food and drink, I'd feel a lot safer. "Would you like a drink? Tea? Coffee? Something cold?"

"Coffee would be great, thanks."

Attempting to fill a kettle with water while juggling a heavy lead doorstopper and fiddling with a cell phone might have worked for a circus clown, but not for me. So, with one eye on Hudson, who'd slumped into the nearest chair, legs apart, shoulders tense, kissable lips completely un-kissable as they narrowed into a thin straight line, I placed my potential weapon on the kitchen sink, still close at hand but out of the way, programmed my phone and continued preparing two coffees. One heavy-duty black laced with half a dozen paracetamols for me and a white with one sugar for the now-silent man sitting at my kitchen table.

"So," I said, my shaky hands causing the cups to rattle together as I picked them up. "You wanted to talk."

He looked up as I placed his coffee on the table in front of him. A wariness taking over from the anger in his eyes. "You're not at all what I expected."

I didn't answer. With hair normally associated with Troll Dolls and crumpled slept-in clothes two sizes too large, there was not much I could say. *I don't normally look like this,* sounded a bit defensive. And I had nothing to be defensive about. Hey, I hadn't invited this guy to my home.

He looked down as Flerken, the traitor, rubbed up against the leg of his faded jeans and snuffled a smiling welcome. The moment Hudson's hand reached out and scratched him behind the ears, Flerken leaped onto his lap. "I was told the police were questioning you as a suspect," he said, his fingers continuing to stroke the ginger fur until the cat curled up, purring, and went to sleep under the logo on Hudson's black tee that read, *Bikers Do it Best in Bed.*

"Who told you that?"

"Mr. McInerny. His family breeds Schnauzers." I nodded in recognition of the man who'd pointed out the Driscoll's camp site. "They can't stand the fact that Dad's dog beats their International import every time they meet in the ring."

"I can see how that wouldn't go down well. Not when they'd be looking to recoup their outlay from the imported dog's stud duties." I sighed. For me, showing Busta was fun. But there were a few jealous competitors, addicted to winning, who smiled on the surface and performed sneaky tricks beneath the folds.

But surely not murder…

"Mr. McInerny also told me you were a bit flakey."

"Flakey?"

The corners of his lips twitched at my freaked-out expression and was that a laugh hiding behind his eyes? "I haven't made up my mind about that one yet."

I frowned. Barely refrained from poking out my tongue. Did I *really* care which way his mind went? I fisted both hands together to stop from patting down my hair again, or tugging the neckline of Abi's black tee up a bit higher. Instead I glared at him. "So…these McInernys," I said, determined to keep to the script, "was their animosity ever more than just a show ring grudge?"

"Don't know. But I've been to the shows with Mum and Dad a few times and there's often heated words exchanged between them."

"Yeah, but I can't see that being a motive to commit murder."

One eye twitched. "Do you read murder mysteries, Molly? Watch True Crime on television?"

I shook my head. Hey, I was a Happily Ever After fan.

"You'd be surprised how a lit match can spark a raging fire in the most trivial of circumstances." Hudson took a sip of his coffee, straightened the colorful bandana around his forehead and then glanced across at me again. "Mr. McInerny also said you found Dad's body."

"I did."

Busta, who'd been lying at my feet, stood up and nudged his nose under my hand, as if to stop me from picturing Harry's dead face again. I looked down, smiled at the shoelace dangling from his mouth, and rubbed his favorite spot behind the ears. He leaned his whole body against my leg.

"He also said you were hanging around near Mum's camp. That you could easily have taken the long-bladed scissors from her grooming kit."

"Whaat?" Careful not to disturb Busta, I leaned forward into

Hudson's space, glared at the three rings in his nose. Overkill. "I barely knew your father. In fact, before yesterday, I'd exchanged no more than ten words with him. And those ten words mainly consisted of hello and nice day."

"Well, why were you seen arguing with him in the cafeteria just before he was murdered?" Hudson's voice ran over gravel. "And before you deny it, I heard that little tidbit from two different sources."

Suddenly this guy didn't seem cute any more.

"And did either of your busybody, blabbermouth sources mention that your father came bolting through the cafeteria like he'd seen a ghost and knocked me completely off my chair? That I ended up sprawled on the floor like loose fruit from an upended basket?" Anger building up inside me, I banged my hands flat on the table and glared at this interloper who'd come into my house, was drinking my coffee, and was now accusing me of murder. "What did you expect me to do, Hudson? Kiss his hand and thank him for my bruises?"

Hudson's frown slid off his face. "That's not like Dad."

"No, it's not. But your Dad was either running away from someone, or in a hurry to meet that someone – *and* he was scared witless." I leaned closer. "Do you know anyone who could have had that effect on your father?"

"Not really." He shook his head slowly. "Naturally Dad's upset a few people in his life. Who hasn't? But I can't think of anyone who would want to murder him." He let out a sigh. Closed his eyes. Suddenly looked younger, more vulnerable. "Maybe it was a random attack. You know, he accidently stumbled on someone committing a crime, they panicked and stabbed him."

"Did he ever mention being blackmailed?' I shrugged one shoulder. "Anyone demanding money to keep quiet about something he did in his past?"

Elbows on the table, head resting on his hands, Hudson frowned. Without speaking, he shook his head.

"No late-night phone calls?"

"Don't know. Haven't lived at home for the last four years. And Dad wouldn't talk about that sort of thing anyway."

"Well, someone frightened him." I thought of the death threat Harry shoved in my jacket pocket. "Wait. I'll show you what I mean."

My denim jacket was hooked on the back of my chair. After I'd promised to drop the evidence off at the police station – today – Abi had stuffed the note back in my pocket. I felt around, yanked out the crumpled paper and placed it on the table. "Your father snuck this into my pocket while pulling me up off the floor. I think it was a cry for help." Before Hudson could accuse me of withholding evidence, I shook my head. "I know, I know, I should have handed this over to the police at the crime scene, but, remember, I was in shock at the time."

His frown deepened as he read the three words, turned the paper over, checked out the back. "This is vital evidence."

"And I'll make sure Detective Lightfoot gets it today." I almost told him about how I'd discovered the paper had been torn from a *Betty Boop* writing pad – but I didn't know this man. Didn't even know if he really was Harry's son. So, I kept quiet.

"Any other hidden clues up your sleeve?"

"No, but I'm determined to find out who murdered your father."

"Why?"

"One, I don't like being a murder suspect. And two, your mother is also a suspect and she's too sweet to be a murderer."

He looked up, studied me more closely and then his frown cleared. "I know who you are. You and your two friends solved Petra Sullivan's murder a couple of months ago." He raised both eyebrows. "You're one of those Chewing Gum Chicks."

I set the growl in my throat to silent. "*Gumshoe Chicks.*"

He grinned. "Like in Private Investigators?"

I shrugged one shoulder. "We started sleuthing in high school. Stolen bikes and a couple of chocolate heists back then, but when Petra was killed, we progressed to murder."

He grew still, eyes solemn, lips tight as he placed one large hand over mine, his woodsy cologne, smelling of fresh earth and pine trees, assaulted my nostrils as he leaned closer. "Molly, I want whoever did this to my dad locked away. For a long, long time." His warm hand squeezed mine and suddenly I had to gulp down a tiresome lump in my throat to make way for air to get through. "But be careful. Anyone who is capable of killing once, can usually kill again." He withdrew his hand to wrap around his cup. Take another sip of his coffee.

Strangely, I wanted to grab his hand and hang on.

Instead, I nodded at the note. "Do you recognize the paper or the printing?"

He read the words again and shook his head. "Poor Dad. What the heck did he get himself into? Who did he rile up so much they decided to kill him?"

"Think, Hudson. It's important. I know everyone likes to believe their parents are infallible, blameless, but as you said, he must have done something wrong." And then I remembered Stephen Channing's cruel words about not blaming Harry for straying when his wife looked like a blob of dough. "What about other women? Was he cheating on your mum?"

Hudson's fingers gripped his cup so tightly I wouldn't have been surprised to see a crack jag down the side. His eyes narrowed as he glared at me. Reminded me of a cornered tiger. "Why? What have you heard?"

"This isn't the time to get all defensive, Hudson. I heard from a certain big mouth at the dog show that your father was a womanizer and he was making eyes at one of the female judges – Lady Rhianna Hamilton-Davies, to be precise." I took a sip of my coffee, regarded the guy with the arresting blue eyes and long fair hair over the rim of my cup. "Any truth in that?"

He slammed the cup down on the table and exploded to his feet. "Yes. And I hated him for what his philandering was doing to my Mum. In his own way, I think he loved her, but he couldn't stop exploring greener pastures, always on the lookout for something prettier to play with." Eyes like flint, teeth jammed together, he shook his head. "And Mum didn't deserve that. She cooked for him, washed his dirty clothes, looked after us kids and now my sister's two kids and...and... "

He came to an abrupt halt, arms in the air, fists tight.

For the first time since I'd let Hudson inside my door, I could actually visualize him killing his father in a fit of rage.

Sons, especially, can be very protective of their mother.

After a lifetime of simmering anger at his father's sexual indiscretions, had Hudson caught his dad playing around with yet another woman at the dog show and reacted by slamming the deadly scissors deep into his father's heart?

5

I was thirteen minutes late for our *Gumshoe Chicks'* meet-up. Not due to Hudson's outburst – he quickly realized he was scaring me and apologized profusely. He even offered to make me a cup of coffee while explaining how he was at an Adult College giving a lecture on Motor bike maintenance, miles away from the showground, at the time of his father's death. Even gave me the phone number for the college, so I could ring, to check out his alibi.

Instead, I blame our tardiness on the time it took to rescue Hudson's soggy shoelace from my cheeky fox-terrier's jaws. Or to then refuse the offer of coffee and steer a reluctant biker out through the front door so I could shampoo and persuade my troll-like black hair back into its normal everyday setting.

Whatever. At thirteen minutes past two, after unbuckling the shoe-lace-thief from his soft leather harness on the passenger side of my lovingly restored 1963 red Morris Mini Cooper, Busta and I scurried through the front doors of Abigail's dog-friendly boutique, *Pampered Pooch*. Both of us, by now, slightly wilted.

The first thing I noticed was Penelope's face. Now, if Penelope had been human instead of the most adorable and patient greyhound in the Universe, she'd be rolling her eyes and sighing dramatically. Instead, she stood immobile, her big brown eyes giving me that martyred, 'it's-okay-she-really-does-love-me' face, as Dana fitted her dog out with a flamboyant watermelon-pink bandana and matching elf-hat. To add to the indignity, the hat came with holes on each side for Penelope's ears to poke through.

"Wattayathink?" Dana looked up from adding huge Gucci dog sunglasses to the outfit and grinned up at me. "Cute?"

"As cute as a headache after four glasses of wine. You're as bad as your Munchkins." I looked around for Kayla and Jake. "Where are they? Don't tell me you lost them on the way."

Dana grinned. "They are currently being entertained by their father. It was a 'bring the kids to work' afternoon at his office."

I let out a giggle at the thought of Peter, Dana's mild-mannered husband, chasing his 3-year-old daughter and naughty 15-month-old son around the office. "That should be a story to tell your grandkids in years to come."

"Personally, I think Penelope looks adorable. That shade of pink suits her," put in Abi bringing the conversation back to Dana's long-suffering greyhound while she stacked half-priced fluffy dog booties that wouldn't last ten seconds on Busta's feet, onto a display table. Beside her, Abi's assistant, Veronique, was adding the final touches to the display. When Abi inherited *Pampered Pooch* from her deceased Aunt Tilly, Veronique actually came with the deal. And Abi always insisted that without her loyal assistant and friend, she would never have succeeded in keeping the doors of *Pampered Pooch* open.

Dana nodded at Abi. "It does, doesn't it? The color brings out the highlights in her eyes."

"So why are you covering her *highlighted* eyes with those awful sunglasses?"

Dana wrinkled her nose at me before perusing Penelope's attire more closely. "Hmm…you're right…too much." She slipped the sunglasses off Penelope's head and stepping over Scout, the Driscoll's giant schnauzer who was stretched out on the floor watching proceedings, returned them to the shelf before addressing me. "Now, Molly, before we get on with today's assignment, have you dropped off the evidence to Detective Lightfoot yet?"

"Mmm…"

"Molly?"

"I was running late so I stuck it in an envelope together with an apology for not handing it in sooner and left the envelope at the front desk with the policewoman on duty. Okay?"

Dana rolled her eyes. Mother of two kids under four she was an expert at getting her message across via an eyeroll. "Detective Lightfoot won't be pleased. He'll want to talk to you."

I hadn't thought of that. What if the steely-eyed detective came looking for me? What if he dragged me off to the police station accusing me of withholding evidence? What if I ended up in a 4 x 2 cell with a steroid-enhanced guy called Boris sporting bad breath, teeth sharp enough to pry beer caps from bottles and a body covered in biker tattoos?

"Nothing pleases Detective Lightfoot." Abi, who'd had past dealings with the difficult detective, broke into my thoughts.

I batted the scary prison image away. Best scenario, if I ended up in jail, I could always use the experience as research for my writing and incorporate the Boris character into one of my future books. "Actually, I'm glad I didn't hand the evidence in sooner. We wouldn't have discovered *Betty Boop*."

"Our only clue," agreed Abi. "Now all we have to do is find the writing pad the paper was torn from."

She made it sound so easy…

I watched Abi collect her cherry-red *Guess* bag with the gold chain strap from under the counter. She slung it over her shoulder and moved across to clip leads on her two dogs, the Driscoll's Scout and her own lovable dachshund, Chloe. "Are you two ready? We're expecting a visit from the Bobbsey twins and their gang of four later this afternoon and I need to be back here to help Veronique cope with the fallout."

"Bobbsey twins?" Dana let out a hoot.

"The two Miss Robertsons," explained Veronique, her lips twitching. "They're elderly sisters who still live in the house they grew up in. And fight? They're like dog and cat. If one picks out a set of red doggy-coats the other one declares she wants blue. And the same goes for choosing worming tablets, doggy-beds, squeaky toys. Whatever."

"And let's not forget the gang of four," Abi put in, eyes twinkling. "Huey, Dewy, Louis and Pumpernickel. All of mixed breed, all over thirteen and all incontinent. Between chasing after the dogs with a damp mop and ensuring The Twins don't resort to poking each other's eyes out, their arrival usually makes for an entertaining half hour."

Veronique nodded. "Followed by a black coffee strong enough to grow hairs on your chin the moment they leave."

"So, unless I'm kidnapped, flattened by a bus, or eaten by an aggressive show judge, I'll be back by four," Abi promised her assistant as she pushed against the front door and stepped onto the footpath.

As usual, due to Abi's big white work-van being the roomiest, we humans piled in the front while the dogs made themselves at home in the back. A tight fit with an extra canine, but it's amazing how dogs' bodies can adapt to small spaces.

"Guess who knocked on my front door today?" I said, fastening my seatbelt while Abi programmed the GPS to the Hamilton-Davies address, before pulling out onto the main road.

Dana raised one sassy eyebrow. "Chris Hemsworth?"

"I wish. No, it was Hudson Driscoll. Harry's son. Or so he said."

"And you let him in?" Abi squeaked. "What if he was *pretending* to be Harry's son? Did he show you any ID?"

I shook my head and opened my mouth to speak but Dana cut me off. "With a murderer on the loose, letting a stranger into your house could have been dangerous, Molly."

"More like crazy," insisted Abi. "What if he'd knocked you out, dragged you into his car and then dumped you over a cliff?"

I blinked at them. "Come on, guys. You'd have done the same thing if he'd knocked on your front door."

Abi's fingers tightened on the steering wheel while Dana found something extremely interesting to study on the front of her jacket.

"I'm right, aren't I?" I said, shaking my head as the penny dropped.

"Maybe," said Abi.

"Only if the kids weren't home," said Dana.

Frustrated, I shook my head at them. "Hey, if I'm going to be a genuine *Gumshoe Chick*, you have to stop protecting me. I'm a big girl now and if I can't participate fully, what's the point?"

"It's not that, Molly. It's just that sometimes you're...I don't know...too nice."

"More like too gullible," added Dana, not one to pull her punches.

"Hey, if he'd looked like a murderer, I wouldn't have opened the door," I told them,

thinking back to how the thought *had* crossed my mind. "But I could tell he was a good guy, just by looking at him."

"What? He had a sign pinned to his shirt saying, '*I'm a good guy, let me in*'?"

"Besides," I said ignoring Abi's last jibe. "I had Busta to protect me."

We all glanced back at the smiling fox terrier currently washing Penelope's face while Abi's dachshund, Chloe chewed on his right ear and Scout, taking up more room in the back than his share, lay there and watched. Fascinated.

I sighed. "Okay. *And* I had Flerken."

"My bet would be on the cat." Dana grinned releasing the tension in the air. She raised one eyebrow in enquiry. "So...what was he like, this Hudson guy?"

What was he like? I couldn't stop the smile or the odd sensations swirling in my stomach as I thought of those arresting blue eyes and long wavy hair, wild from the way he kept running his fingers through as he tried to keep himself from falling apart. "Okay. I guess."

"Ah! Ha!" Dana leaned closer. "You have a look in your eye that tells me Hudson Driscoll has a lot more going for him than, 'okay, I guess."

I let out another sigh. Hudson might be a looker, but he was so not my type. He had 'player' written all over him. With his black leather, his wild shoulder-length hair and gym-enhanced muscles, he reminded me of that A-hole Gray, from my current romance. So why was I attracted to him? Why couldn't I stop thinking of him? Especially as I'd been brought up to settle for nothing less than commitment, a ring and wedding bells in the future.

"Well, come on, what did he want?" Dana persisted.

"Just to talk."

"And?"

"He's the youngest of the family, around 29, single, several nose rings, rides a Harley Davidson and reminds me of Gray, the protagonist in my current novel, 'The Love Triangle.'

"But?"

"But he also has a motive for killing his father."

Both Dana and Abi's heads swiveled to face me.

"Well, don't stop there," said Abi before quickly looking back at the road. "What motive?"

By the time I'd finished telling them about Harry's infidelity and how it was making his wife's life a misery and his youngest son possibly murderous, we'd turned into Jacaranda Avenue, Walkerton, where the Hamilton-Davies lived.

Well named, a canopy of purple Jacaranda trees grew on each side of the road. Large well-cared-for houses lined the street, some gauche in their newness, some over a century old and built to last another hundred years.

We stopped in front of number 82 and while Dana and Abi were quick to disembark, I hung back. Did we really have the right to question these people? And how was the volatile show judge going to react when she spotted me?

Busta wanted in. He batted me on the arm, all smiles, but after winding the window a quarter-way down for air, I told him he was safer in the car.

A huge rambling house, big enough to accommodate two or maybe even three families, the Hamilton-Davies home was typical of houses built by the moneyed class in the early 1900's. It sported a well-tended garden, two manicured-lawn tennis courts and a well-equipped pool set behind a recently constructed spikey iron fence.

After extricating myself from the safety of the car, I followed Abi and Dana along a diagonal path, up a flight of six steps and onto a large shady wrap-around veranda.

"Ready?" Dana looked at me. "The moment Rhianna answers, I want you to shove the checkbook under her nose. That way she won't slam the door in our faces. No one, especially the rich, ever refuse the offer of money."

When I nodded, she lifted the heavy brass knocker and banged it against the thick elaborately carved front door. A door that could have been incorporated on a movie set in a castle in Medieval England.

I glanced over my shoulder at the little sharp-nosed canine face pressed against the car window. No way should I have brought Busta with me. What if the judge saw him? What if she carried out her threat to neuter him? I sighed, told myself to grow a spine. Rhianna Hamilton-Davies wasn't going to touch a hair on my dog's back.

I wouldn't let her.

After a short wait, Dana knocked again. This time for longer and with more force.

"Hmm," said Abi, nose plastered to what was probably either a front bedroom or lounge room window. "Seems like no one's home."

I blew out a sigh and slipped my checkbook back into my bag. I'd post it to her instead.

"There's two cars in the driveway so there has to be someone around." Dana moved across to join Abi at the window. "Let's wander around the back. Our well-heeled couple might be enjoying afternoon tea or a glass of champers with caviar under the patio."

With another glance at Busta, whose head was now poking out over the top of the window, I followed Dana and Abi along a narrow cement path around the side of the house. Manicured bushes, perfectly shaped trees and a garden ablaze with color surrounded us. Either one of the Hamilton-Davies had an energetic green thumb or they employed an expensive full-time gardener with a degree in Horticulture.

Loud strident voices could be heard coming from around the corner of the house, somewhere in the vicinity of the backyard. A man and a woman, shouting, snarling at each other. So obsessed in their tirade, their exchange of insults, it was little wonder they'd failed to hear Dana knocking on the front door.

"Hang on, let's wait here." Dana came to a sudden halt, eyes alight with anticipation. From our hidden position at the corner of the house, we had a bird's eye view of the two warring participants. Rhianna Hamilton-Davies, the show judge, and her Mayoral husband, The Honorable Michael Davies. "We don't want to burst into a domestic, do we?"

I stifled a grin as we hunched down out of sight. More like we wanted to hear what was going on in case it helped with our investigation.

"You *stupid* woman." It was the Mayor, his voice spitting venom as he loomed over his wife like a snake poised to strike. "How could you be so obtuse? How could you allow yourself to be blackmailed?"

"I didn't *allow* myself to be anything, Michael." Rhianna tossed her head, evidently not fazed by her husband's spit and threatening bluster. Or she was past caring. "I discovered the note under the door when I arrived home from my Book Club meeting, ten, fifteen minutes ago."

"If you behaved with the decorum and dignity of a Mayor's wife, instead of chasing tail all over town like a harlot from the wharves, there'd be nothing for a blackmailer to latch onto." A dapper but daunting man, he glared at Rhianna, his face a twist of ugly.

She laughed in his face. "And you're a saint? What happens when that giant ego of yours gets a little bruised? You can't keep a lid on your temper, that's what. You turn into the Incredible Hulk. So, Michael, how do we know the blackmail note isn't for you?"

"Don't be ridiculous!"

"No more ridiculous that you saying it's for me."

"Who's it from?"

"How should I know? It's not signed. All it says is…"

And that's when Busta, in full-on, exuberant fox-terrier mode, appeared on the scene.

He streaked past us, a flash of white and brown in hot pursuit of a blurred smudge of feline gray. Energized by the chase, Busta's barking grew shriller, more frenzied, as he closed in on his prey. Round and round the garden they ran, dog and cat, uprooting flowers, toppling statues, frightening goldfish, until, with the knowledge of home territory, the cat finally took refuge in one of the perfectly pruned trees and immediately gave his adversary the finger, via a hiss of displeasure that included slit eyes and curling lips.

"Busta! Come here!" I tried to yell but after standing with my mouth open, watching the destruction of the Hamilton-Davies' perfect garden, the words came out as a croak.

However, he must have heard. With another volley of barks, probably to inform the cat exactly what would happen if he ever had the pleasure of chasing him again, Busta trotted over to me. Tail wagging, a smile on his lips. Almost like he'd performed a star Vaudeville act and was waiting for the foot-stamping and applause from the audience.

"Go! Go! Go!" I yelled, the first to come to her senses and realize it wasn't only Busta who needed to make a run for it. We humans were also in deep doo-doo. "Sorry," I shouted over my shoulder to the open-mouthed combatants as I hot-footed it back to the car with the other two *Gumshoe Chicks* breathing down my neck. "I'll pay for the damage."

"Damn," said Abi hurling herself behind the wheel and turning the key in the ignition.

"Double damn," I said letting Busta leap into the car before checking over my shoulder and, finding no loaded shotgun pointed in our direction, sliding in beside Abi.

"Two more minutes," grumbled Dana slamming the car door behind her as Abi hit the accelerator and screeched off down the road. "Just two more minutes and we'd have found out what was written on the blackmail note."

"Yeah," I agreed and let out a sigh. "And maybe if either of those two had anything to do with Harry's murder."

6

"He said *what?*" Veronique tossed hair from her eyes and glanced up from draping a large multicolored felt caterpillar over the back of the squishy sofa Abi had set up in the boutique for customers and their canines. With so many exciting goodies on display, shopping at the *Pampered Pooch* could sometimes be a tiring experience.

Abi nodded. "Yep. Our Honorable Mayor, called his wife a 'stupid woman'" – she put the two words in air-quotes with her fingers – "and then likened her to a harlot from the wharves."

"Harsh…"

"And his wife likened *him* to The Incredible Hulk."

'Why?"

"Due to his violent temper, I guess."

We'd arrived back at the *Pampered Pooch* in record time, tumbled out of Abi's white van and were now in the process of recounting our adventure to Abi's eager assistant, Veronique.

"And *one* of them is being blackmailed?" Abi continued; eyes alight as she watched Veronique's mouth drop open at this juicy piece of news.

"But we don't know which one." I shook my head at Busta who was busy washing his new friend, Scout's, ears with an ultra-exploratory tongue. "Thanks to one extremely naughty fox terrier, we didn't get to hear what was actually on the blackmail note."

"It was so funny, though." Abi let out a giggle. "You should've seen that puss go. He was just a blur of fur hurtling around the garden with Busta right on his tail. And when he scuttled up the tree and gave Busta the finger, I almost wet my pants."

I blew out a sigh. "Not going to be so funny when I have to return to the scene of the crime, check-book in hand, and pay for all those damages."

"There is a bright side, though. It will give us an opportunity to dig around a little, maybe find out why they're being blackmailed," put in Dana checking her watch for the third time in the last ten minutes. Due to managing her own mobile dog wash business, *The Hydro Hound*, plus investigating, she was often late collecting her two offspring from Day Care. In fact, Dana's name had been written up on the Naughty Mummy's Bulletin Board twice in the past week. However, by the way she was keeping tabs on the time, she'd decided that it wouldn't happen again.

"Might pay to leave it until they've calmed down a bit." I gulped at the thought of not only facing the Hamilton-Davies but also the high cost of paying for the damage to Rhianna's expensive boots and now her even more expensive garden.

"It'll give us a chance to ask questions about her affair with Harry."

Eyeing Dana under my lashes, I shook my head in total bewilderment. "How do you come out and ask a person you barely know if she was having it off with Lizzie Driscoll's husband? The guy who ended up dead in his own trailer with a pair of grooming scissors deep in his chest?"

"Easy," said Dana, looking smug. "Just appeal to her vanity. Point out how her husband doesn't appreciate her amazing qualities. That she must be beating men off with a stick. And then, carefully slide in the fact that you heard she and Harry Driscoll were an item."

I could feel my mouth gape in awe as I listened to my friend's clear logic. Dana Fox should be a counsellor or a psychologist. "Wow! So, when we return to the Hamilton-Davies household, you, my friend, will be our designated speaker. You'll be in charge of the mission, while Abi and I will merely watch, listen, and learn."

Abi nodded. Evidently as impressed as me by Dana's knowledge of the human psyche.

"So, do you think this has anything to do with Harry's death?" Veronique straightened the pillows on the couch and flopped down, sinking into the squishiness of the fake leather. She leaned back and kicked off her shoes. Clearly eager to rest up while the shop was quiet and to hear more.

"What else could it be? A coincidence?" I collapsed on the couch beside her. The stress over Busta's carnage eventually hitting home. "Don't think so. A blackmail note gets shunted under their door the day after Harry's murder. Nope. Someone saw something important at the showgrounds. Maybe even saw who ran the scissors through Harry's heart."

"And it seems that 'someone' intends to bleed the murderer dry." I shook my head. "Trouble is, blackmailers never know when to stop. They just keep asking for more and more money."

Veronique nodded. "Until they end up being added to the murderer's body count."

"Sorry, gotta go." Dana, snatched up her voluminous, many-pocketed shoulder bag that must have weighed a ton. She clicked her fingers at Penelope who immediately scrambled up and attached herself to Dana's side. "Can't give that snobby-nosed Patricia Stamford of the *Canberra* Stamfords another chance to gloat. If she calls me a bad mother one more time, I'll have to hurt her and that would get Kayla and Jake kicked out of Day Care and me trying to bathe dogs with one hand while changing my son's nappy with the other." She reached down to snap a lead onto Penelope's collar before rushing toward the front of the shop. "Okay with you two if we meet outside the Mayor's house at 10 o'clock tomorrow morning?"

"Veronique?" Abi threw a raised eyebrow in her assistant's direction.

"Go for it. Tuesday morning's normally quiet anyway."

Knowing I could wake up at five and finish my daily word count before leaving, I nodded, "Fine by me. But remember, *you* do the talking, we do the listening."

"Gotcha!"

As Dana pushed through the glass doors, Penelope glued to her side, two identical elderly women, wizened, stick thin, and accompanied by a rag-tag bunch of dogs, doddered into the shop. Steel gray hair scooped back into wispy buns, tortoiseshell spectacles, long dark colored skirts, black stockings and ill-fitting blousy tops; the two women could have somersaulted straight from the pages of a school history book.

The Bobbsey Twins?

While Abi smiled a greeting, Veronique heaved herself off the couch, slipped on her shoes and headed in the direction of the mop bucket. Already the rattiest member of the gang of four had made his mark on the lacquered floorboards.

"We'll have four packets of liver treats please," said one of the twins, her voice loud enough to blister paint.

"No, no, no. We'll have four packets of *lamb* treats," insisted the other, sharp pointy chin jutted in determination.

"Liver."

"Lamb."

"Liver."

"Lamb."

"Why not two of each?" Abi suggested, smile cemented in place. "And while you're here, ladies, come and take a look at these gorgeous soft doggie booties. Just arrived from the U.K. yesterday. Amazing quality, and guaranteed slip-proof." Abi, like the Pied Piper, led the two warring sisters away from the array of dog treats and over to the newly arranged display of dog booties. "These are selling like hot cakes, ladies, so, knowing how your little fur-babies have trouble with their pads, I put four sets aside for you. Just in case."

The most alert of the four dogs, furless across his back end, feet splayed, and arthritic legs struggling to hold him up, blinked one owlish eye in the direction of Busta and let out what he probably thought was a challenging woof but actually sounded more like a death rattle.

I leapt off the couch and grabbed Busta by the collar to prevent him returning the greeting. Geez, one welcoming lick from Busta and the other dog's legs would splay so wide they'd get stuck in the splits position – and leave me paying vet bills, on top of replacing Gucci boots and returning the Mayor's garden to its pristine Home-and-Garden Magazine condition.

Unable to physically say hello, Busta let out a volley of barks, tail wagging like a wigwam at a railway crossing. If my dog was human, he'd be the guy in the bar who'd shout everyone a beer. The guy who collected friends like others collected stamps. Smiling, my fingers took a stronger hold of his collar.

"We'd betta go, Busta," I told him and reached out with my other hand to hook my bag over my shoulder.

One of the Bobbsey Twins, the one who preferred lamb treats, shook a wrinkled finger in Busta's direction, the leather handbag over her arm jiggling in agitation. "That dog is a menace. He's vicious. Out of control."

Busta smiled at her.

And that's when the smallest of the gang of four, an unusually shaped terrier/spaniel/Pomerium cross with large flyaway ears, let out a gigantic rumbling fart that sent a stomach hurling smell throughout the store. He then squatted next to a display of pink and gray *Oh! Banana* dog pajamas, and followed through.

"Oh! My! God!"

Leaving Abi and Veronique to reach for face masks, scented sprays, mop bucket and the pooper scooper, Busta and I shot through the front doors like we'd been invaded by a zombie apocalypse.

On the way home, while driving along the familiar highway, radio softly playing country in the background, my mind wandered to the male protagonist in *The Love Triangle*. Should I give Gray several nose rings, like Hudson? A cheeky dimple? A smile that rocked a girl's world? Nah. Maybe a couple of ear studs and a beard. That was enough. I had to forget about Hudson Driscoll. Like Gray, he was trouble. Bad boy trouble. Certainly not the hero I'd imagined for *my* future.

I let out a sigh and turned the music up a little higher. Listened to some woman with a voice like a squeaky shed door, lament about the one who'd got away. Who was I kidding? I was no giftbox myself. I was weighed down with neurosis, had trust issues, lived through my fictional characters and could barely say two words to a guy making a pass at me without tripping over my own tongue.

What normal man would want to tick all my extraordinarily high boxes? A priest? A Saint? The most boring man in the Universe?

Was that who I wanted to spend the rest of my life with? A man who was so rigid, so uptight he wouldn't know how to smile, to laugh at adversity, to have fun?

It wasn't until I turned the corner of my street and drove past the cottage with the gray and white shutters and pretty rhododendron bushes, that I noticed a police car parked like an exclamation mark right outside my unit.

Immediately, my throat closed over. I struggled to breathe. What was a police car doing outside my address? Were they there to arrest me for withholding evidence?

My first thought was to turn the car around and speed off in the opposite direction. Keep going until I was in the next state. But when one of the policemen, a burly guy with several day's growth and what looked like a cache of weaponry strapped to his belt, stepped out of the car, settled his police hat firmly on his head and held up one hand, palm outward, I came to a reluctant stop beside him.

"Ms. Molly Gibson?"

"Yes."

"Earlier today, did you leave an envelope at the front desk for Detective Lightfoot?"

"Y-yes." Oh, God, I knew it! They were going to lock me up, with no laptop, no Wi-Fi, and only a toilet-roll on which to finish writing, *The*

Love Triangle.

"Detective Lightfoot wants you to accompany us to the station to answer some questions."

I gripped the steering wheel like it was the last lifebuoy in a sinking ship. "B-but I can't come now. I mean, I haven't written my word count for the day. And-and I'm behind in my deadline."

For answer, the stony-faced cop opened the back door of his vehicle and made an ushering movement with one hand. "Ms. Gibson, ma'am, I'd like you to park your car, take care of the dog and then get into the patrol car."

When I merely blinked at him, his eyes, like the jagged rays of a lightning strike, narrowed into slits. "Or the next thing I'll be doing is loading you into a prison cell!"

7

Detective Lightfoot's office looked different from the last time I'd visited, a few months ago when Dana and I had accompanied Abi to the police station. At the time, Abi was keen to share a clue with the detective in regards to the Petra Sullivan murder.

On that day, I could have left any time I wanted.

Today, if I went to walk out, I'd probably end up in handcuffs.

Which is why the room seemed colder, grayer, more unwelcoming. The smell claustrophobic. Even the clock on the back wall I'd thought rather cute when viewing it the first time, now appeared grim. Who thinks it funny to show numbers shaped like cartoon prisoners on a clock dial with two sledgehammers for the hands?

Detective Lightfoot, the Big Kahuna, the man seated on the other side of the desk from me – that's who.

"Give me one good reason why I shouldn't arrest you for withholding evidence, Ms. Gibson. Why I shouldn't lock you up and throw away the key." He held up the note for my perusal. "This is an important piece of the puzzle. Surely you must have realized that."

I leant forward in my chair, remembering to keep eye contact like they advised in all those articles on self-confidence I'd read in waiting-room magazines. "I'm sorry, Detective. I was in shock. I'd just witnessed my first dead person. *And* there was blood." I shivered and wrapped my arms around my upper body. "You might regard finding dead people as passé, old hat, but my brain went walkabout the moment my eyes landed on those blood-stained scissors. In fact, I was still trying to process the words *dead* and *Harry* in the same sentence when you came along and battered me with questions and accusations. I just freaked. All I wanted to do was get as far away from the crime scene as possible. Go home. Get my brain rewired. Try to forget."

"And it took twenty-four hours for you to do that?"

I let out a sigh. Nope. The man would never understand.

"Why didn't you bring this death threat to my attention the moment you remembered it was still in your jacket pocket?"

I let out another sigh. Felt my shoulders sag. This wasn't going well. Obviously, I couldn't admit I'd got drunk, spent the night on Abi's couch, and didn't wake up until midday today. Wouldn't look good on my prison resume.

"If it's any consolation," I said, eye contact front and forward again. "By studying the death threat, a little longer, I was able to come up with a clue."

"Miss Marple to the rescue?"

Snarky *and* ageist. I bit my bottom lip to prevent myself from informing him I was so not a Miss Marple. I was 28 years old – not 68. I was more a Nancy Drew. And proud of it. "Do you want to hear my theory or not?"

"I'm all ears."

More snark. I gritted my teeth. Thought about what I could do to a character like Lightfoot in my next novel. I'd make him suffer. Give him a lover who not only cheated on him but maxed out all his credit cards, scratched the sides of his classic Lamborghini with a nail file, dipped his toothbrush in the toilet and added itchy powder to his talc.

I smiled. Yeah, that felt much better. "Well," I said, stashing the smile in case he mistook it for friendliness. "Right on the edge of the paper, where its torn, you can just make out the word *Boop*."

The detective picked up the evidence, frowned at the paper and then slowly shook his head. "And?"

"I figured it's been torn from a *Betty Boop* writing pad."

"Oh, right. So, all we have to do is procure the names of the thousands of people who've ever bought a *Betty Boop* writing pad and check their alibis for the time Harry Driscoll was killed." He rolled his eyes. "Do you realize how ridiculous that sounds?"

If I'd been a balloon, I'd have deflated, floated around the room making farting noises and finally plunged to the ground, a useless piece of waste material.

"Did you see anyone near the dog trailer when you were talking to Mrs. Driscoll, before you found her husband's body?"

I shook my head. "The trailer was a little away from where they'd set up camp. Plus, there were some bushes blocking the view."

"Was Mrs. Driscoll nervous? Acting suspiciously?"

"She was worried because Harry was running late to exhibit Scout, their giant schnauzer. She said that wasn't like him at all. He usually had the dog groomed and ready to go in the show-ring well before time. That he never left it until the last minute. So, yes, she was nervous. She was worried that something had happened to him." I sniffed, felt my bottom lip threaten to quiver. "And she was right to worry, wasn't she?"

Lightfoot nudged a sterile white tissue-box in my direction. The look on his face plainly told me what he thought of criers. "And you went to the dog trailer on your own?"

I sniffed again but refused to reach for a tissue. "My friend Dana offered to show Scout for Mrs. Driscoll, so I went to the trailer to collect his ducky." The detective hiked both eyebrows. "The dog gets excited and shows better if he plays with his ducky before going in the ring." The eyebrows didn't lower. I let out another sniff before adding, "Evidently."

He shook his head, sighed, and then booted up his computer. "I've decided not to charge you for withholding evidence, Ms. Gibson, but this is definitely my last warning to you and your nosy amateur sleuth friends. Leave the investigating to the police. Right?"

I immediately did my bobble-headed dog routine and smiled at him.

Ignoring my smile, the detective consulted his computer. He tapped on a few keys and regarded me over his long aquiline nose. "How long would it have been from the time Harry Driscoll slipped this note into your jacket pocket until you found his body in the trailer?"

"Um…a little over half an hour, I guess."

"And he left via the back door of the cafeteria?"

I nodded.

"Did anyone follow him out?"

Thinking back, I frowned. "Well, I'm not sure. I watched Harry leave by the back door, but then I was sort of distracted by picking up my chair and settling in front of my laptop again. I guess someone could have followed him." I shrugged, shook my head. "But I didn't see them."

"We have two witnesses who saw you arguing with the deceased–"

"I wasn't arguing. He knocked me off my chair…"

"And *they* noticed someone follow him out of the cafeteria."

My ears pricked up and waggled.

Still reading from his computer screen, Lightfoot narrowed his eyes. "But one witness maintains the stalker was a man in shiny black shoes, his face covered by a dark hoodie while the other witness insisted it was a woman wearing a raincoat with a hood and in long red boots." He blew out a sigh and shook his head. "Probably neither. Only last week we had three different witnesses swearing they saw a clean faced teenage boy throw a brick through the window of a jewelry shop. Turned out to be a 70-year-old man with a beard that would rival Santa Claus."

But I wasn't listening.

At the mention of long red boots, my heart stopped its normal rhythmic *kerplunk kerplunk*, coughed, spluttered and restarted in a frenzied feverish hyper hip hop break-dance beat.

Had Rhianna Hamilton-Davies been lurking in the cafeteria hiding behind a hoodie when Harry came barging through? Had she been waiting for him? And as soon as he left, followed him to his dog trailer and killed him?

8

Two minutes to ten and Dana was a no-show.

Sweat gathered on my forehead and under my armpits. I sat hunched in my little red car outside 82 Jacaranda Avenue, Walkerton, a cold block of ice lodged in my chest. How could we confront the show judge, and possible murderer, Rhianna Hamilton-Davies, about her indiscretions without the logical but feisty member of our team present?

Abi, whose van was currently at the auto repair shop for its annual service, swiveled in the passenger seat beside me and patted my arm. "Don't worry, Dana's just running late. Jake probably lost his doggo and you know how he carries on when that happens."

Which was true. Jake refused to leave the house without his ratty stuffed toy dog. Patched, darned and laundered so many times it was now faded to an indeterminable gray color, Doggo was never far from Jake Fox's dimpled baby hands.

My phone dinged as a text came through. It was from Dana. Fumbling in my haste, I clicked to read the message: 'At the Children's Hospital. Jake swallowed Kristoff from Kayla's Disney's Frozen Castle Village Lego set. Best scenario he'll poop it out. Worst, they'll have to go in.'

"Poor Jakey!" Abi leaned across to read from my screen.

Another text popped up: 'Do not abort plan. Think positively.

Imagine Rhianna in nothing but fishnet stockings, knee-length boots, and a funny hat. Nothing like a half-naked woman to slam her down to your size.'

Tamping down my nerves, I flipped a text back: 'Will do. All the best with Jakey. Bet Kayla's going spaz at losing Kristoff.'

'You're not wrong. Tell me again why I thought it was a good idea to have kids?'

'Because you love them.'

'If you say so. Now go chomp the lion in her den. Gotta go. Jake gone red in the face. Maybe Kristoff's about to be liberated.'

"Kids!" Abi slowly shook her head as she read the texts. "Always wondered why my womb was allergic to them. Now I know. It's called self-preservation."

Me…I was what you'd call, sitting on the fence about wanting kids. One side of the fence went all gooey when I saw a gurgling baby in a pram and the other side got all creeped out at the noise that issued from one end and the unrestrained bodily fluids from the other.

"Okay, looks like it's just you and me, Molly." Abi opened the car door and swung her feet out onto the footpath. "So, let's do it."

Not the words I wanted to hear.

She stood up, stretched both arms in the air and then twisted her body from side to side. "Small cars like this were designed for fairies and frogs. Too cramped for humans."

"I like it," I said reluctantly joining her on the footpath. "This car makes me feel secure and loved. It's homey. Comforting. Like being wrapped in a warm soft blanket."

The eyeroll Abi sent my way said she thought I was talking a load of bollocks. But I wasn't. My classic red Morris Minor, lovingly restored by the nice man from the corner of my street who'd died and his widow had to put the car up for sale two years ago, was my pride and joy. Suited me fine. Why did I need to drive a family-sized 4-wheel drive when my family consisted of Flerken, Busta and me? And Flerken never left the house.

"Did you bring a check to pay for the Gucci boots?" Abi, who'd set off along the path toward the house's Medieval front door glanced over her shoulder at me.

I nodded. Too stressed to answer. My mind a blank on how to introduce Rhianna's supposed affair with Harry Driscoll without detonating World War III and bringing the ceiling crashing down on my head.

Abi grasped the heavy bronze knocker and banged it against the door several times, the dull thud reverberating through the house.

"What I'd like to know," I said bouncing from one foot to the other, "is how Dana knew the Hamilton-Davies would be home at this time of day?"

Thinking back, our illustrious leader had been quite specific with the day and time when arranging this meeting.

"Dana has connections," Abi said. "While traveling from one house to the next, hydro-bathing and grooming dogs, the owners talk to her, confide in her, divulge all their secrets. Not only that, they divulge the secrets of everyone else in the dog show world."

I frowned. "But how does that answer my question?"

Abi lifted the knocker and let it fall on the door again. "That's how she learned the Mayor and Mayoress throw their home open to their constituents every Monday morning, from 10.30 to 11."

"But it's only ten o'clock."

"So, we're early." Abi shrugged. "Don't want anyone bursting into the middle of our conversation, do we?"

The door opened a few inches and a sickly-strong smell of pine after-shave, hovering around a jowly face that was trying hard not to scowl, peered out. "Open House doesn't start for another half hour, ladies."

"Good morning, Mr. Mayor." Abi slid her foot into the space between the door and the jamb and sent the scowling Mayor one of her megawatt smiles. "We're actually here to see Rhianna, in a personal capacity. Also, my friend here, checkbook in hand, wants to apologize and pay for the damage her dog did to your garden yesterday."

His scowl deepened and his eyes, gimlets of fire, swung around to incinerate me. "So, you're the owner of that flea-bitten mongrel that wrecked my garden."

Refraining from advising him that the words *mongrel, fleas* and *Busta,* were an oxymoron, I nodded.

He turned back to Abi. "What the hell were you and your friends doing on my property yesterday? And why'd you run off?"

"Um…why did we run off?" Abi looked like her mind was blanker than a sheet of paper with not a pen in sight.

"Because my dog's crazy," I said digging deep into my imagination while hoping Busta never learned of my betrayal. "He's under veterinary care, you see. And when he gets over-excited, like he did yesterday, we have to get him home pronto and dose him up with his pills. Otherwise, he can become quite dangerous."

The Mayor harrumphed and opened the door wider. "You'd better come in then," he growled, then took off down the passageway, still grumbling.

Phew! That was close. Abi sent me a grin and we exchanged eyerolls before tagging along behind.

"Rhianna!" The yell, loud enough to chase birds off their nests two blocks away echoed down the passage. "The owner of that crazy mutt from yesterday is here to see you." When his wife didn't immediately materialize, like a rabbit from a magician's hat, he let out another roar. "Try dragging yourself away from the mirror for five minutes, woman. No amount of make-up will change the way you look."

Rhianna Hamilton-Davies, hair immaculate and clothes definitely not off the peg from the local Target store, appeared from a room further down the passage. "Darling, just because the visage that sneers back at you from your mirror each morning reminds you of a hippopotamus that's smashed face-first into a rock wall, is no reason to get jealous of my naturally good looks."

"Take these ladies into the office and deal with them quickly. My supporters will be arriving in twenty-five minutes." The Mayor, clearly accustomed to exchanging acerbic barbs with his wife, ignored her comment and reached up to straighten his tie. "I added up the damage done to our garden last night. You'll find an account sitting on the desk."

Rhianna rolled her eyes and I half-expected an upright middle finger to follow. "Men!" she growled and then without another word, minced off, confident in her high heels. Abi and I tagged along behind, through an archway into a large dining room – traditional long table set for two – and out the other side to a narrower passageway and finally through the doorway of a smaller room, which was obviously an office.

"Please, sit." Her voice was gravelly as she indicated two uncomfortable looking chairs set in front of a beautifully preserved antique desk. Chairs made of hard wood with sharp edges. Chairs that were definitely not indicative to long friendly chats. Then, once we were seated, she strutted around to the other side of the desk and sank into a luxuriously upholstered office chair.

"Now," she said her eyes narrowing to slits. "What are you two *really* doing here?"

"Um…" Abi cleared her throat, put on her best goody-two-shoes face. "We're here so Molly can pay for the damage to your garden."

"Is that so?" Rhianna's voice ran over more gravel. "So, why were you and your other friend, Dana Fox, snooping around in my garden yesterday? I don't remember inviting the three of you to my house."

Abi glanced at me again to let me know her mind was still a blank canvas and if I had a pretty picture up my sleeve could I please just jump in and sketch away.

"We thought we saw an intruder."

Abi did a bobble-headed nod.

"A big scary-looking guy dressed in a black overcoat. And – And we followed this guy into your garden hoping to catch him and ring the police, but then your cat sort of spat at my dog and while we were watching the resultant chase, we – er – we lost the intruder."

Abi's mouth fell open while I gave myself an A+ for plotting on the fly. Hey, I wasn't a top-selling romance writer for nothing.

Then Rhianna began to slow clap. "Full marks for ingenuity," she said, picking up a sheet of paper from the desk. She looked over it at us, her eyes snake-like. "But I'm onto you, so watch your step. Bones can easily get broken when you trip up."

Abi licked her lips, eyes on the window as though contemplating escape.

I shivered, let my eyes drop to my hands which were clasped in my lap. Gripped so tightly they'd gone numb and my skin white, bloodless.

"Now, down to business." Rhianna smiled, then perused the paper in her hand for a few moments before passing it across the desk to me. "This must be the account my husband referred to. Seems pretty fair."

I pulled myself together, stared at the numbers at the bottom of the account. And blinked. That couldn't be right. "$10,000?"

"That's the cost of replacing the plants and bushes ruined by your dog, plus the workable hours calculated by our landscaper to bring the garden back to its original beauty."

"Um…" I gulped down a lump in my throat. I'd need to sell a lot of books to cover that amount. "Maybe I could do the replanting myself…"

Rhianna didn't speak. Didn't have to. The expression of horror on her face clearly said, 'I'd rather be staked out naked on an ant-hill than allow you to take one step in my garden'.

"How hard can it be to stick plants in the ground?"

"Non-negotiable."

I sighed. "Right. I'll have my accountant check this out and if he agrees with your estimation the money will be transferred to your bank account by the end of the week." Defeated, I sent a silent message to Abi who was fidgeting on the hard chair beside me. Okay, these chairs were uncomfortable – probably descendants of the ducking stools used to indict witches in the Middle Ages – but surely, she could see I'd done my share. Surely, she realized it was up to her to continue with the investigative questions now.

Instead, Abi lifted one eyebrow and unobtrusively jutted her chin in Rhianna's direction as if to say, 'Go on – what are you waiting for?'

Okay. I could do this. Summoning up my inner Xena, I stared at the woman on the opposite side of the desk. What were Dana's words of wisdom? To picture my opponent wearing nothing but fishnet stockings, knee-length boots, and a funny hat.

Well, as Rhianna was presently seated, the fishnet stockings and long boots were out of sight so all I had to imagine was a funny hat – oh, yeah, and large naked boobs.

I concentrated on the funny hat. Imagined a tall ungainly red and white striped top hat from Dr. Seuss's *The Cat in the Hat*. Perfect. Tipping to one side in abandon, the hat looked ridiculous on the Mayoress's head. Just the thing to take my mind off the boobs fore and center below.

"So, Rhianna," I said, eyes glued to the invisible hat. "Were you having sex with Harry Driscoll, the guy who was murdered?"

Abi kicked me on the shin. Pain shot up my right leg. Rhianna's Dr Seuss hat toppled off her head and I bit my tongue. Damn. That came out wrong. Nothing like the persuasive words Dana recommended. Something about appealing to her vanity, beating men off with a stick, or was it she was a beautiful woman and…

I gritted my teeth, risked a nervous glance at the woman on the other side of the desk. She was laughing. Laughing so hard I expected her to cough up a hair ball.

"Me and Harry?" she spluttered. "Harry and me? For God's sake, I couldn't stand the pathetic little man. He was a dweeb. Always hanging around like a bad smell and making fish eyes at me. Creeped me out big time. In the end I told Michael to have a word with him. Explain in simple language that if he didn't stop stalking me, I'd cut his heart out and use it as a doorstop."

"A-and did you?" Abi's voice was reed thin.

"Did I what?"

"Try to cut his heart out with a pair of grooming scissors?"

As I waited for her reply, I transferred my weight to the balls of my feet, primed for a quick getaway if things turned ugly. Okay, we'd added Rhianna's name to our suspect list, but hadn't given any thought to what we'd do if we discovered she was the killer and we happened to be alone with her at the time of our exposé.

Rhianna folded her hands on the desk in front of her and leaned forward. "It was a throwaway line, that's all." She shook her head and sighed. "Look, for some reason Harry Driscoll believed he was God's gift to women, when in actual fact, he was a castoff from the 80's. The man had no class. He wore home-knitted cardigans, parted his hair on the side and followed me around like a drooling love-sick puppy. Even left me dreary presents that I immediately binned." She screwed up her nose in remembrance. "Like two-dollar blocks of chocolate from the supermarket. Disgusting stuff. Full of ghastly additives, like glucose syrup, invert sugar, humectants, emulsifiers, hydrolyzed milk protein and maltodextrins." She gave an exaggerated shudder. "The guy was driving me nuts. I had to stop him." She must have noticed Abi's ashen face because she quickly shook her head. "But not by killing him. Okay, I admit, a pair of cement boots and a deep river might have flittered across my mind for a couple of seconds, but the plan was if Harry didn't stop pestering me after Michael warned him off, I'd contact the police and get a restraining order taken out against him."

Poor misguided Harry. Even though he'd been cheating on his wife, I felt a frisson of sympathy for man. Pretentious hungry women like Rhianna Hamilton-Davies always belittled common men like Harry. Had done throughout history.

I studied the woman on the other side of the desk. Was she telling the truth? If Harry continued to harass her, both Rhianna and her husband, the Mayor, had a motive for murder.

And what about the witness who'd seen a woman in long red boots tail Harry when he left the cafeteria a short time before he was murdered? Was Rhianna that woman? Only one way to find out.

I leaned forward in my chair and deposited a check for $1200 on the desk. "This is to replace your Gucci boots. I'm so sorry Busta ruined yours. My fault entirely. I wasn't paying attention at the time. If I had been, it wouldn't have happened." I watched her expression as I continued. "By the way, did you manage to remove the stains?"

Rhianna looked up from examining the amount on the check and shook her head. "Didn't get a chance. The stench of urine was making me sick, so I took the boots off and wore a loaned pair of shoes for the rest of the day."

"Who loaned you the shoes?" I leaned forward in my chair. Maybe there was a reason for talking Rhianna into removing the boots.

She shrugged her impatience. "Does it matter? I'm not expected to remember competitors' names. I judge the dogs, not the handlers." She frowned. "Might have been someone from the non-sporting group. Anyway, when I went back later to collect my boots, they were gone. Evidently someone with light fingers took a fancy to them."

Abi and I exchanged a quick glance.

If Rhianna was telling the truth, she wasn't the woman seen lurking in the cafeteria wearing red boots. Which made me think – did whoever murder Harry steal the judge's boots with the sole purpose of framing her?

Maybe. But was Rhianna telling the truth?

At that moment the door shot open and the Mayor burst into the room, a picture of scowling frustration. The door shuddered as it slammed against the wall. "Rhianna, where the hell did you put my new Burberry cufflinks?"

"In your sock drawer, Michael."

"Not there. I checked."

"Did you try moving your socks a few inches and looking underneath?"

"For God's sake, woman, the Stanton-Worthington's will be here at any moment and I can't find my cufflinks."

Rhianna clambered to her feet and glared at her husband. "God gave you two eyes so you could take care of yourself, not just for counting money and ogling women's boobs." She turned to us and sighed. "Be back in a minute to write out that receipt."

"Why haven't you finished up in here?" Michael grumbled as he followed her out the door.

"If you were capable of changing your own nappy, I would be."

The moment their argument faded, Abi, like a greyhound from the traps, was up on her feet and around the other side of the large mahogany desk.

Horrified, I watched her yank open the top drawer and begin rifling through the items inside. "Abi, what are you doing?"

"Searching for the blackmail note."

"But what if–"

"Come on, Moll. No time for what-ifs. I'll check the desk drawers while you poke around in the bookshelves. Won't take Rhianna more than a few minutes to find Michael's cuff links so this is our only chance."

Abi was right. We wouldn't get another opportunity. Couldn't very well break into the house when the Hamilton-Davies were out. Or could we? I shook my head. What was I thinking? Breaking and entering wasn't part of my makeup. I'd been brought up to not only respect the law but to be afraid of it.

Ears on speed dial for signs of Rhianna's return, I scurried across to the bookshelves which covered one entire wall and began pulling out random books, shaking them to see if a note was hiding amongst the pages, then returning the book to the shelf.

From behind me I could hear bangs and curses as Abi seemingly drew a blank with each drawer she searched. "Damn. No blackmail notes in here," she loud-whispered. "Maybe they tossed it in the fire."

"More likely one of them hid it in the drawer beside their bed."

I was almost at the end of the first row, and knowing I'd never check all these books before the Mayoress returned, fumbled in my haste as I pulled out *Fifty Shades of Grey* – they owned the three-book set which was no surprise – and the book slipped from my hands, crashing to the floor, spine first.

I immediately froze. Any minute Rhianna or her pugnacious husband would come charging through the office door, phone in hand, ratting us out to the police.

"Hey, what's that?" Abi pointed at the book lying open on the floor. "There's a sheet of paper poking out from the middle. Quick! Check it out! See if we've hit paydirt."

While Abi almost tripped over a chair in her hurry to get out from behind the desk, I scooped up *Fifty Shades of Grey*, slid the paper from the pages and returned the book to the shelf.

Then, with Abi's breath hot on my neck as she peered over my shoulder, we read the note together:

'I KNOW WHAT YOU DID. PUT $500,000 CASH IN THE LITTERBIN NEXT TO THE FOUNTAIN AT PETTIGREW PARK 2PM TOMORROW OR YOUR SECRET WILL BECOME FRONT PAGE NEWS.'

"That's today." I glanced at my watch. "And the ransom drop is in precisely three hours and twenty-nine minutes."

"But what did they do?" wailed Abi staring in frustration at the words on the paper. Words that gave no hint of the crime. Merely, 'I know what you did…'

"Surely it has to be about Harry's murder."

"It's the only thing that makes sense. Harry was murdered on Saturday and this note gets shoved under their door on Sunday." Abi pulled out her phone. "Here, hold the note up so I can take a photo."

Raised voices could be heard in the passage outside the door.

"Quick!" I whispered, my voice more croak than speech. "That's Rhianna coming back. No way can we let her catch us with this!"

Suddenly the blackmail note turned into a red-hot branding iron that was burning my fingers.

If either Rhianna or the Mayor opened that door and caught us in the act, we were officially dead meat.

9

"I nearly wet my pants when I heard them outside the door," said Abi, ten minutes later as we sped along Port Road, towards Abi's house.

"If it hadn't been for the arrival of Mr. and Mrs. Stanton-Worthington, both dripping money like they'd been caught in a shower of hundred-dollar bills, we'd have been the smashed avocado on their breakfast toast."

A cold shiver had me gripping the steering wheel more tightly. When the door of the office cranked open, I'd been holding the blackmail note in the air while Abi took photos on her phone. But Rhianna didn't come in. It was the knock on the front door and Michael's blustering insistence that they both welcome the illustrious couple that stopped her in her tracks and saved us from being caught out.

We didn't hang around.

After returning the note to the middle pages of *Fifty Shades of Grey*, (a book I noticed was awash with fire-engine red highlights) we'd called it quits and baled, smiling manically at the Mayor, Mayoress and their wealthy constituents on the way out.

"You know," I said, thinking back to our latest ordeal. "Rhianna didn't appear worried when I queried her about sleeping with Harry. Just disgusted. If she murdered Harry, would she have joked about cement boots and a deep river?"

"Maybe it was her way of putting us off the scent."

"But she wasn't that fussed when I asked her about the red boots either. If she'd followed Harry into the cafeteria wearing those boots, you'd think she'd have been more flustered."

"Women like Rhianna never get flustered. They have brass balls. They can lie or joke themselves out of trouble without breaking a sweat." Abi gulped. "But did you see her face when she was slow-clapping and then casually remarked how bones can break when you fall over?"

I nodded. "She knows we suspect her of killing Harry."

"And was sending us a not-so-subtle warning to butt out."

I still couldn't add two and two together and come up with a sensible four. "But why would she kill Harry when all she had to do was contact the police and slap a restraining order on him?"

"Maybe it was to do with prestige. You know, being the Mayor's wife, she didn't want the Media prying into her affairs, so decided to get rid of the evidence – Harry." Abi shrugged. "And for all her bravado, that husband of hers would be scary to live with. Think how he'd react if the Stanton-Worthingtons or any of his other wealthy constituents thought his wife was a slut."

She had a point

"Expecting a visitor?" I asked raising my eyebrows as we neared Abi's house.

Abi frowned. There was a powerful motor bike – a Harley Davidson to be exact – parked in her driveway. She studied the bike through the car window as I pulled up. "Don't know anyone who owns a Harley." She wound the window down and poked her head out for a better view. "And I don't know the guy using the walls of my front porch to prop himself up either."

I switched the engine off and leaned across Abi to see for myself. "That's Hudson Driscoll, Harry's son. What's he doing here?"

"The guy you've got the hots for?"

"Do not."

"Do so."

"Do not."

"Do so."

Oh, God, we sounded like the Bobbsey Twins. Refraining from continuing such a childish argument, I opened my car door and stepped out onto the road. I still wasn't sure about Hudson's involvement in his father's death and had no intention of driving off and leaving Abi alone with the man.

And maybe there was a small part of me – just a smidgen – that was looking forward to seeing the leather-clad biker again.

"Hudson?" I said watching his lithe body unfold from where he'd been squatting on Abi's porch. "What are you doing here?"

"Come to check on Scout. I'd take him home myself but my landlord has a thing about pets in units. Says it sends his insurance bill sky high." He put a hand out to Abi. "Hi, I'm Hudson Driscoll."

Abi shook his hand. "Molly told me all about you."

Hudson lifted an eyebrow in my direction before turning back to Abi. "I'd like to personally thank you for taking care of Dad's dog. I'm hoping it won't be for much longer. At the moment Mum's a basket case. They've taken her in for more questioning. Someone – probably a tire-kicker – reckons they saw her in the vicinity of the dog trailer not long before Molly found Dad. Mum swears she hadn't been near the trailer since they'd finished setting up camp down the hill and under the tree." He shook his head. "It's total chaos at home."

Abi patted his arm. "Scout's no trouble at all and my dog, Chloe, absolutely adores him, so he's welcome to stay with us until your Mum's back on her feet." She slotted the key in the lock, pushed the door open. "Want to come in and say hello? He was a bit mopey this morning. Probably missing his family."

Hudson stepped back to allow me to enter after Abi. "How'd it go at the police station when you dropped off the evidence?"

"As badly as expected. Still, I'm here and not locked up, so I guess that's a big plus." From the backyard I could hear little sausage-dog yaps and a cacophony of loud big-dog barks. "Think your mate knows you're here."

The moment Abi opened the back door a large black furry flash, tongue lolling to the side, smile plastered across his face, lunged at Hudson. The dog's body twisted itself into corkscrews in an impossible attempt to climb up into his arms. Hudson knelt down on the floor and the two embraced. "Love you, buddy," he said both arms wrapped around the black furry giant. "I hope you're being a good boy for Abi. She's a nice lady and you have to take care of her. Okay?"

The dog rested his large intelligent head on Hudson's shoulder, brown eyes soft, and sighed. Hudson sighed with him. "It's one big mess, isn't it boy?"

Looking down at Hudson, all I could see was a guy who'd lost his father in the worst possible way and was now in danger of losing his mother to a mixed-up justice system. Surely neither Hudson nor his mother were capable of murder. My gut instincts said no way and so did the Hamilton-Davies' blackmail note. Resisting the urge to run my fingers through Hudson's long hair, I scrubbed my hand over the top of Scout's head and scratched behind his ears instead. "We have some information that might help clear your mum."

He gently pushed the dog down and stood up. "I'm all ears."

"One of the Hamilton-Davies' is being blackmailed," I told him. "Not sure about the who but I'm pretty sure I know the why."

"What does the blackmail note say?"

Abi pulled up the photo she'd taken on her phone, passed it across to Hudson. "Doesn't say who or what, but like Molly, I think it's to do with your dad's murder."

Hudson took Abi's phone and studied the photo. "And you found this in the Mayor's house?"

I nodded. "Shoved in between the pages of *Fifty Shades of Grey*."

"Woah. And are we going to follow it up? Stake out the park at 2pm today to see who does the pickup and follow them?"

"Why not?" We hadn't got around to processing that part yet, but it was the next logical move. "We just need to bring Dana up to date first."

"Looks like we can do that right now," said Abi, peering through the lounge room window. "Dana's 4wheel drive is pulling up out front. And Jake's with her, so he must have ejected Lego Kristoff the natural way." She turned to me with a grin. "Now, there's a story Jake can tell his grandkids when he's old and gray."

By the time Dana, Jake, Kayla and Penelope, their greyhound had reached the front porch, Abi had thrown the door open. "Hey, Jakey," she said, giving him a high-five. "You okay, little guy?"

Kayla, Jake's three-year old sister, dressed in the cutest pair of *Frozen* jeans and matching tee-shirt, held up a Lego action figure for Abi's perusal. "Jake swallowed my Kristoff. Now Kristoff's really sad." She dropped her bottom lip and gave Abi 'the look'. "Here, Aunty Abi, kiss my Kristoff better."

I let out a smothered giggle. Kayla was Abi's god-daughter and she found it almost impossible to refuse the little girl anything. But knowing where Kristoff had been over the last few hours, there was no way she was going to put him anywhere near her lips.

"Go on," urged Dana sweeping through the doorway with a grin. "Safe as houses. He's been thoroughly fumigated, sterilised and decontaminated." Her grin widened. "I dare you."

Abi kissed her middle finger and placed it on Kristoff's Lego nose. "Glad you made it through the other side, bud," she told the action figure before whipping Kayla up into her arms and swinging her around until she had her giggling hysterically.

After depositing Jake on the floor with Doggo, his favorite toy, Dana turned to Hudson, gave him the once-over and then lifted one appraising eyebrow. "Abi, are you going to introduce me to the hot guy standing in your kitchen, or am I going to assume he's a vision of my imagination?"

"That's Molly's new friend, " said Abi with a smirk.

"He's Harry's son, Hudson," I said feeling warmth radiating from my cheeks. I've never understood why God made it even harder for shy people to overcome their shyness by making them blush so easily.

"I'm Hudson Driscoll," said Hudson, returning Dana's appraising eyebrow with one of his own. "And I'm guessing you're Dana, the third member of the Chewing Gum Chicks."

Dana held out her hand. "Pleased to meet you, Hudson. But if you call us the *Chewing* Gum Chicks again, I'll have to hurt you."

Hudson grinned. "Point taken."

Dana nodded and turned to me. "So, how did it go at the Hamilton-Davies? Anything to report?"

It was now less than three hours before the scheduled drop-off at the park – time to fill Dana in on our latest news. "We found the blackmail note."

"You did?" She lifted one eyebrow at my hesitation. "And that's good isn't it?"

I sighed. "But we have no idea which of the Hamilton-Davies' it was intended for, or even if it has anything to do with Hudson's dad's murder."

"But we know the where, the time and the amount of the ransom drop." Abi held up the photo on her phone for Dana and Hudson's perusal. "All we have to do is be close by so we can follow the blackmailer when he or she picks up the money."

"Good work," said Dana lifting a squirming Jake away from Scout's large teeth which were currently fastened around one of Chloe's squeaky toys. "And did you interrogate Rhianna about sleeping with Harry?"

I grimaced as Hudson's face fell. "Sorry, Hudson, but yes, I asked her and she thought it was a huge joke."

He sighed. "I'm afraid my father *was* a huge joke."

"But he didn't deserve to be murdered," I added, squeezing his hand, "which is why we're going to find out who stabbed him."

"Thank you." Hudson returned the squeeze and then folded his arms across his black leather jacket and straightened his shoulders.

"Okay," said Dana, taking control while handing Jake and Kayla a juice box each from her oversized carry bag. "Firstly, we can't rock up at the park together. That'll put the Hamilton-Davies and the blackmailer on alert. So, we arrive separately. Find somewhere close enough to the litterbin to establish who makes the drop-off, but far enough away to avoid suspicion. You, Hudson," she said pointing at the newest member of our investigative team, "lose the biker look, wear old clothes and bring a bucket and a broom handle with a nail on the end to pick up trash or an industrial sized broom for sweeping. Today, you're a park cleaner. Okay?"

Hudson blinked, sent Dana one of those *wtf* looks she deals with on a daily basis and then nodded.

"And Abi, call Nathan and arrange to meet him at 1.45 for a picnic in the park. Take sandwiches, a thermos of coffee, and a blanket. Make it look cosy and intimate. Right?"

Nathan Forrester was Abi's boyfriend. He was also a busy PI. How Abi was supposed to get Nathan to agree to a picnic on such short notice was anyone's guess. But Abi and Nathan's relationship was still at the lovey-dovey, I'll-do-anything-for-you stage, so she had that going for her.

"And you," Dana continued, nodding at me. "Go home, change into something more writerly, grab your laptop, find a park bench that's within sight of the drop-off point, and work on your manuscript." She shook her head. "But try not to get too involved with your characters…right?"

I'd be better off compiling a grocery list. If I got involved with Gray and Tabitha's current dilemma, I'd be in another world when the blackmailer showed up and still be sitting on the bench hours later when the park officially closed for the night.

"What about you? What are you going to do?" Abi, squatting on the floor next to Kayla and an open make-up box, lifted one blue-clad eyebrow. Her brightly painted lips, compliments of her god daughter, were slightly parted, showing several lipstick-covered teeth.

"The kids and I are going shopping for a kite. They've been pestering me to go kite-flying for weeks now, and although we won't officially be taking part in this mission, I think today is the perfect time and Pettigrew Park the perfect place for such a family-friendly activity. Don't you?"

Kite flying might be a family friendly activity, but for the rest of us, this plan had no family friendly seal of approval. We were going to stake out a ransom drop-off and then track the blackmailer to his hidey-hole.

But what Dana had forgotten to mention was what the heck we were supposed to do with this alleged blackmailer if and when we caught him, or her. What if the blackmailer was armed? And what if he or she recognized one of us while he or she was being chased?

I blew out a troubled sigh. There were far too many *what-ifs* in this plan for my liking. After all, I was more comfortable with neat, ride into the sunset, happy-ever-after endings. As for mystery – that was *so* not my genre.

10

*G*ray *tugged her hard up against him and kissed her, his mouth tasting of bourbon and salty peanuts, his 10 o'clock shadow rough against her cheek, His hands were everywhere. They moved down her back and cupped her bottom, drawing her even closer to the pulsating erection under his zipper.*

"No," she said pulling back and grabbing air in her constricted lungs. "This is a huge mistake, Gray. You're everything I don't want in a man. You're a biker. You're trouble. You're a one-night-stand kind of guy. Ethan is the man I love. He's rich, smart, connected, going places–"

"And he left you at the altar."

Tabitha sighed. Yeah, there was that.

After twelve months planning a wedding for a thousand guests, constant phone calls to the caterers, swanning around the most exclusive boutique wedding shops in Adelaide and Melbourne trying on wedding gowns, Ethan had dumped her in front of a toffee-nosed priest and a thousand tittering guests. Before the wedding there'd been articles written about them, photos in women's magazine of her standing next to Ethan, his arm draped around her. And what about the one hundred beautiful pearls she'd hand-sewn into the wedding-dress from Heaven she'd finally chosen. A dress costing more than she'd earn in a year.

With always the thought at the back of her mind...why me? Out of all the well-connected beautiful women abounding in Ethan's circles, why had he chosen a plain-Jane admin. assistant from his Law firm. A woman with–'

"Aunty Molly," a small sticky hand planted itself on my cheek together with drool from whatever lolly Kayla was currently sucking. "Mummy said to tell you to stop writing. She said you'll miss the drop." Kayla tipped her head to one side and frowned her innocent three-year-old frown. "Is something big and bad and scary going to drop out of the sky, Aunt Molly?" Her baby blues opened wider. "A monster?"

I dragged myself back to *this* reality and shook my head. "Um…no darling, it's just an expression. Nothing's going to drop from the sky. You can go back and tell Mummy I said I'm on it."

After the little girl skipped back to Dana, Jake, and the ugly dragon-like kite they were struggling to keep aloft due to the fact that there was no breeze, I saved and closed the document I'd been working on and opened a boring financial page on Excel – a page full of numbers my accountant insisted I save for him. I wriggled into a more comfortable position on the park bench. Numbers should keep my attention focused on the green metal litterbin set on the side of the path instead of poor spurned Tabitha's tangled emotions.

I could see Abi stretched out on a plaid travel rug beside her hunk of a boyfriend, Nathan Forrester, dark eyed and smoother than vats of Haigh's chocolate. If they didn't stop eyeing each other like the dessert menu at a posh hotel, they'd miss the drop too.

I grinned. Kayla was on her way over to break up the lovefest, courtesy of her ever-vigilant mother. Dana and her kids might not be taking part in this mission, but boy, Dana was still in charge. Any minute now Nathan and Abi would receive a much-needed wind-up call, courtesy of the sticky-fingered touch of Dana's three-year-old emissary.

I twisted around on the park bench, searching for Hudson, the remaining member of our investigative team. Pettigrew Park encircled me, its lawns, shrubs and trees stretching away in the distance, walking paths, public barbecues, a kids' playground on the left. I could hear the flute-like warble of a magpie, strutting around like an emperor after digging for earthworms nearby. The shrill cries of girls and boys climbing ropes, being pushed on swings, running, laughing, playing chasey, and the reality of why we were stationed here at the park, a place of fun and serenity, waiting for a ransom drop by a blackmailer, slammed me in the gut. Was I really cut out for this way of life? Of calling myself a bona fide *Gumshoe Chick*? What if I crumbled when confronted with danger? What if I didn't have the necessary backbone in a crisis and caused one of my friends to get hurt because of my insecurities?

And then I spotted Hudson. My heart quickened. And for some reason, I felt stronger, more confident. Hudson was pushing a straw broom, sweeping leaves into a pile on a path not far from the litterbin. Was he too close? Would the Hamilton-Davies recognize him when they made the drop? Unlikely. Hudson didn't handle his dad's dog in the show ring, and just like Gray in *The Love Triangle*, he didn't mingle in rich and famous circles. Park cleaner clothes suited him, but made me wonder exactly what my new biker friend actually did for a living. Motor bike mechanic? Tattooist? Drug dealer?

Nah, his face was too honest to make it as a drug dealer. I smiled across at Hudson as he swept leaves from the path. Instead of his usual black leather, helmet and gang-related insignias, he wore workman-like jeans and a long-sleeved flannel checked shirt with a Crows cap turned around the wrong way. My smile widened. The park-cleaner clothes made him even more yummy. In fact, when he bent over to bag up some leaves, I felt drool settle at the corner of my lips as his blue jeans tightened impressively across his fit derriere.

Hudson looked up, saw me ogling him and winked. Blushing, I shifted my gaze back to the spread sheet on my computer. No matter how fine Hudson's backside might be, he was not my type. He was a biker. He was a babe magnet. He played rough. Maybe if I wrote that down one hundred times, like when Gran made me write 'I must not associate with boys', a hundred times, the day she caught me sitting in the dirt playing marbles with a boy from school when I was ten.

At that moment, Rhianna Hamilton-Davies, wearing a designer track suit, extra-large sunglasses and an enormous hat that shaded her face, came strolling down the path toward the litterbin. In one hand she carried a nondescript gray plastic bag and in the other she clutched a dog leash with a tiny miniature black poodle on the other end. Her husband, the Mayor, was nowhere in sight.

So, Rhianna was the one being blackmailed. And the snarky laughter and sneer of disgust at being accused of sleeping with Harry was all fake. Maybe she *had* slept with Harry, he'd insisted she leave her husband to be with him and when she refused, he threatened to let the world know – so she had to silence him.

Arriving at the arranged drop, the heritage green metal litterbin, Rhianna slowed, took a covert glance over her shoulder, and then casually leant up against the bin while surreptitiously edging the bag full of money inside. She then tugged the little black poodle away from the base of the bin where he'd been busy leaving his mark, and retraced her steps.

Once she was out of sight, I glanced across at Abi and Nathan. They were up on their feet, plaid blanket folded on the ground, sandwiches and thermos returned to Abi's bag. Nathan had casually propped himself against the trunk of a tree and tugged Abi to him. Outwardly, they were just another young couple kissing, cuddling, making-out, impervious to anyone around them. But even from a distance I could see their shoulders were stiff and knew they were both alert for action.

Dana had gathered Kayla, Jake and their uncooperative dragon kite and relocated to the anomality of the playground where she could still direct the action while keeping her children safe. Already Jake had commandeered the best swing in the park, while Kayla, left thumb planted firmly in her mouth, stood watching three little girls take turns sliding down the slippery dip.

I looked across to where I'd last seen Hudson and frowned. His straw broom was lying on the grass verge beside a mound of dead leaves, but Hudson was nowhere to be seen.

Had he gone to the bathroom? Was he following Rhianna? Or had he decided to set himself up by hiding behind a bush closer to the litterbin?

A cold chill crept up my spine and lodged in my chest. Or had the blackmailer, on the way to the drop-off point, twigged that Hudson was spying on him and decided to rub him out of the picture?

My hands shook as I closed my laptop, slipped it into my bag, and stood up. I wiped sweat from my eyes and moved in the direction of the abandoned broom. If Hudson was in trouble, I needed to be there for him.

Hurrying across to the pile of leaves, I picked up the broom and stared at it, as though the inanimate object could tell me where Hudson had gone, what happened to him and why he'd disappeared.

And that's when I saw what looked like a man wearing a tracksuit and a faded black hoodie hitched up around his face riding toward the drop-off point on an e-scooter. As he passed the litterbin, he casually leaned over and scooped up the bag of money, and then, without slowing down, continued on the path.

Nathan and Abi immediately unlocked lips, scrambled away from the tree and set off after him. Their plaid blanket, hats and picnic basket forgotten.

I stood clasping the broom, mouth open, watching the e-scooter turn a corner in the path and disappear from sight.

No way would we catch this guy. Not when we were on foot. The blackmailer was aboard an e-scooter capable of travelling at 30ks an hour? What had we been thinking? That the blackmailer would casually stroll through the park on his walking-frame, lift the money from the bin, count it out, and then totter on, smelling the roses as he went?

A roar from behind set my heart catapulting against my ribs. I spun around, heart pitching wildly, to be confronted by Hudson, once again dressed in his black leather jacket and biker's helmet, astride his motor bike. He came to a stop beside me. "Hey, Molly," he yelled over the noise of the motor, "if you can bear to part with that broom, hop on behind me and we'll do what they say in the movies and 'follow that e-scooter'."

I shook my head at him. "It's 'follow that cab', not 'e-scooter', and I-I've never been on a motor bike before."

Motor bikes are unladylike, dirty, and lead to depravity – the Gospel according to Great-Granny Teresa.

"Hey, rinse your mouth out with soap, girl. *This* isn't a motor bike. *This* is a Harley. A freedom machine. An adrenaline-fest. Ride on one of these babies and it'll blow your mind wide open." Hudson's voice was reverential. "And all you have to do is sit tight and hold onto me." He unhooked a spare helmet and tossed it across. "Now, let's move it, babe, or our blackmailer will have flown the coop."

The roar grew louder as Hudson revved the accelerator impatiently. The bike juddered, lifted its front wheels off the ground like a temperamental thoroughbred at the start of a race.

I rammed the helmet on my head, fastened the strap and snatched a quick fortifying breath, praying for courage as I eyeballed the lethal 'freedom machine' – did I really want my mind blown 'wide open' – then, flinging my leg over the pillion seat I wriggled into position and grabbed at Hudson's jacket.

"Put your arms right around me, Molly, and hang on tight. Don't want to waste time scraping you up from the roadway. We might lose our target."

"Glad you've got your priorities right, Driscoll." My laptop lodged between us, I wrapped my arms around Hudson, enjoying the warmth and the ambiance of the muscles moving under the leather. This could be fun. The bike reared, gave one almightier growl for the chase, I let out a scream, and we took off, scattering pedestrians from the path like confetti.

Around the bend and half-way down the track, we found Abi who'd slowed to a plodding walk. Her face was a plum shade of red and her hair sweaty strings of drool. Might be time for the *Gumshoe Chicks* to implement that exercise class we'd been talking about for the last six months but hadn't got any further than checking out the bods on the instructors at a local gym, online. If we were going to continue with our investigations, we needed to be more streamlined, more capable of the physical side of catching bad guys.

Abi pointed to a path up ahead that branched off the main track. "The blackmailer went down there," she gasped. "Nathan's – puff – still following – puff – but no way can we catch the e-scooter on foot."

I gave her a thumb's up and almost lost my balance as the Harley surged forward.

A hundred metres along the second path, we came across Nathan, head up, arms pumping, moving at a fast jog. I eyed him with envy. If that had been me, I'd be bent over, hands on knees, trying to catch my breath.

We *Gumshoe Chicks* definitely needed to get ourselves to a gym. And soon.

"Couldn't maintain the speed," Nathan told us as he jogged along beside the bike, his pullover tied around his waist. "Should have realized the blackmailer wouldn't be on foot. Careless error. But be careful, there's a mob of schoolkids up ahead. Looks like a school excursion. You'll need to slow right down. Whoever was on the e-scooter didn't and from back here, it looked like they barely missed knocking into one of the kids."

I peered over Hudson's leather clad shoulders and immediately spotted what Nathan was on about. Up ahead, a shamble of children – possibly hundreds but probably no more than fifty – were running in every direction, screaming and jumping as though they'd finally escaped from the classroom and were determined to enjoy every second of their freedom. In amongst the chaos, two distraught teachers, one waving her arms and yelling for silence, the other blowing a shrill tin whistle that likely set every dog in the neighbourhood howling, were striving to bring the mob under control. Both looked like they'd rather be home scrubbing the bathroom floor with a toothbrush.

"Damn." Hudson slowed the Harley to a crawl, finally coming to a stop beside the whistle-blower. "Excuse me, Ma'am, but did anyone wearing a hoodie and riding an e-scooter pass through here?"

"Are you illiterate?"

"Excuse me?"

The whistle-blower drew herself up to her full height of five foot nothing and scowled at Hudson. "The signs state that no vehicles of any kind are to be ridden in the park. And yes, an idiot riding an e-scooter steamed through here a couple of minutes ago, came close to knocking over one of our children." She gripped the Harley's handlebars with both hands and her scowl deepened. Unless we ran right over her, we were going nowhere. "E-scooters have no licence plates, but motor bikes do, so if you don't get off and walk this vehicle out of the park immediately, I'll report you to the police."

"Er, I don't suppose you noticed anything about the person riding the e-scooter?" I said. "You know, male or female? Old or young? Bald or hairy? In fact, anything at all would help."

When she didn't answer, merely put the whistle to her lips, I scrambled off the back of the bike so fast I accidentally elbowed Hudson in the chin. Hey, I didn't want that woman blowing her whistle anywhere near my ear.

By now Nathan had jogged up beside us. "Everything under control here?"

"Yes, thank you," the whistle blower told him, her scowl indented into her forehead as though it had been carved there with a chisel. "The biker and his biker chick are going to walk their dirty piece of metal out of the park while I stand here and watch them."

I almost swallowed my tongue. Biker chick? Me? Wow!

Hudson growled low in his throat. "Dirty piece of metal?"

"So…no luck identifying the blackmailer?" Nathan said to us.

Hudson turned off the engine and climbed off his Hog. "Nah. He's well and truly scarpered – but not before he almost took out one of these kids. Another black mark against him."

Nathan nodded. "You know, what we need is more ammunition in our belt. How about I do a background check on each of our suspects."

"You can do that?"

"I can uncover information about a person's associates, assets, court history, business interests, employment, financial problems and–"

A whistle sounded in my ear. A whistle so shrill it probably peeled the lining off my eardrum. I frowned at the short dumpy teacher who believed she was God. "Hey, lady, would you stop doing that? You'll send us deaf."

"You're already deaf. I told you to move that bike out of the park, yet it's still here."

"Okay, okay, Whistlin' Winnie." Hudson shook his head as he removed a bouncing munchkin from the pillion seat of his bike and deposited the child safely on the ground. "No need to get your knickers in a twist, we're leaving now."

Whistlin' Winnie's glare inched closer to freezing point.

Nathan laughed. "See you back at the drop-off point. We can arrange a time to meet at my office from there." He waved and took off at a rhythmic jog.

"Try to soften Dana up for us," I called out to his departing back. "When she sees us returning without a blackmailer by the ear, she won't be happy."

"Don't worry, she'll be apples."

Apples? Nah, I knew Dana better than Nathan and could have told him she would be more like lemons when she found out we'd lost the blackmailer, but figured it was always best to let people learn their own lessons. Instead, I trekked behind Hudson, who was pushing his bike in the opposite direction.

"Once I get the Hog out onto the road, I'll give you a lift back to the entrance gates," Hudson said. "Then, if you like, after we check with the others, I'll drop you off outside Nathan's office."

"Um…okay."

I'd hitched a ride to the park with Dana in her four-wheel drive and was saying yes to a lift to Nathan's office via Hudson's Harley?

I shook my head. Was I out of my mind? I'd only known Hudson Driscoll for 24 hours. He was astride a badass motor bike with the rev capacity to blow my mind. I should be tagging along with Nathan, jogging back to the security of Dana and her four-wheel drive.

Although, on the other hand, Hudson was sort of cute and no way would I keep up with Abi's gym-hardened PI. He was too far away already. I reached out and rubbed my hand over the Harley's shiny rear chrome fender and decided to take a chance on the hot biker striding out in front of me.

I quickly caught up and, grabbing the handlebars on the opposite side, helped propel the bike through the gates and out onto the road.

I'd actually started to look forward to another ride on the *freedom machine.*

A few minutes later, when we re-entered the park, after leaving the Harley out the front, I could see Jake and Kayla playing on the swings while Dana, Nathan and Abi stood talking, heads together, beside the green metal litterbin.

"What's up?" I said, walking toward them.

Abi held up a white silk handkerchief. "Found this under the bin. It wasn't there before the pick-up so we figure the blackmailer dropped it when he leaned over for the money."

"Could be anyone's."

"Take a look at the initials," said Dana.

"And the insignia in the left-hand corner," Abi added.

I took the silky white handkerchief from Abi's hand and studied it.

Sure enough, there in the left-hand corner was the Walkerton Town council crest. A magpie.

And the initials M H D were inscribed diagonally in navy blue lettering in the right-hand corner.

But that didn't make sense.

I squinted at the initials on the handkerchief again, frowned, lifted both eyebrows at my two best friends. "But why would the Mayor blackmail his own wife?"

11

As I climbed the stairs to Nathan Forrester's office, I could hear shrill yaps and squeals coming from behind the wood and glass door at the top.

That'd be Mimi, Nathan's Pomeranian. An uncontrollable ball of fluff originally owned by Petra Sullivan, the victim of a vengeful murder and the first of the *Gumshoe Chicks* investigations. Being a dog lover and fellow dog show competitor, Abi rescued Mimi, the angry little dog with no manners, when she lost her owner and was in danger of being euthanised due to her behavioural issues. But did Mimi appreciate Abi's kindness? Not if you counted the number of times she embedded her needle-sharp teeth in Abi's ankle and refused to let go. It seemed like Mimi blamed Abi for Petra's desertion. Then along came Abi's hunky PI boyfriend, Nathan, and the happily-ever-after of this sad tale is that Mimi fell instantly in love with Nathan – and he with her.

I opened the office door and immediately Mimi came bounding across the room, tail wagging, little crocodile teeth barred in a welcoming smile.

A smile? I goggled down at the sharp-nosed ball of fluff. Mimi didn't do smiling. Her repertoire only consisted of biting and snarling, followed by more biting.

Nathan, ensconced behind his large chrome desk, laptop open in front of him, looked up and his eyes went soft. "Mimi. Time for bed."

The little fluff ball gazed adoring over her shoulder at Nathan before trotting across to a deep fluffy dog bed set up in the corner of the office. I'd seen one just like it displayed in Abi's boutique and its price tag could have been attached to the latest iPhone.

"Good girl, Mimi."

No wonder Abi was in love with this guy. Not only was he a hunk – he was a dog whisperer.

"Hey, Nath, you're a magician, or should I say, a dog whisperer," I told him before lifting one eyebrow at Abi who was busy setting out plates of baked goods on one end of Nathan's desk. "I remember when you couldn't even get that dog's teeth out of your ankle by bribing it with bacon."

She screwed her nose up at me. "Don't rub it in."

Nathan smirked and sent Abi a hot grin which I'm sure would have developed into something more if I hadn't been standing right there. "Can't say I blame the dog," he said with a wink. "Abi's ankle *is* irresistible." He glanced down at Mimi, stretched out on her bed between a colourful stuffed caterpillar and a black and white panda three times her size. "Mimi and I have an understanding. When she's a little ray of sunshine, we're best mates. When dark clouds hover, we stop talking." He tossed a liver treat across to Mimi which she caught in her mouth. "It's almost all sunshine now."

It was my first visit to Nathan's workplace and somehow, I'd expected his office to be a little darker, dingier, like you read about in old PI novels. Instead, his office was modern, professional, but welcoming.

I watched Nathan tapping away on his keyboard while Abi filled the coffee machine with water. They'd been together for just over three-months now and he was the best thing that had happened to her. The way they gazed into each other's eyes, even Blind Freddie could see they were meant to be together. Like I wrote in my romance novels, Abi and Nathan were definite 'soul mates'. I whooshed out a long wistful breath. Would I ever find my soul mate? A man who looked at me as though I was the jewel in his crown, whose eyes lit up like sparklers on a dark night as I approached, who was there for me on a bad day as well as the good. Or would I end up one of those boring old forgotten ladies, loved only by the stray cats in the neighbourhood?

So far, my longest relationship had lasted two weeks, and that would probably have finished sooner except the guy broke his leg skiing and didn't try to force himself on me until his pain meds had fully kicked in. I sighed. And the shortest was half an hour. I'm not proud of that one. A good-looking guy picked me up in a bar, I thought he was really into me, you know, we discussed our mutual enjoyment of rom com movies, Australian history and books by Milly Johnson, but when I refused to 'follow him up to his room' he immediately ditched me and hooked up with an inebriated cheerleader type.

I dropped onto the chintzy sofa up against one wall. A comfortable but out of place cottagey-type sofa which I had a feeling Abi had a big hand in purchasing. I guess she figured it was much more comfortable for snogging than the upright clients' chairs that went with the desk.

With snogging in mind, my thoughts turned to Hudson. And the way he'd nonchalantly reached over and kissed me when he'd dropped me outside Nathan's office. For once, the part of me that shut down whenever a guy got too close, hadn't surfaced. In fact, after having the wind in my face, the feel of Hudson's strong body hiding beneath all that black leather as I wrapped my arms around him, and the rumbling power of the bike under me, I was ready for that kiss. But not for its effect on my heart. Even now, when I thought of those wind-blown cold lips sweetly touching mine, my heart did a back flip with a twist.

I put both hands up to cool my burning face and blinked away the thought of Hudson's kissable lips – he wasn't my type – and watched Nathan's fingers fly over the keyboard on his computer. "We stopped at the *Flour and Icing* bakery to buy these," said Abi dragging me out of my lip-locked daydream. "Figured we needed cake with our coffee. Read somewhere that sugar stimulates the brain."

"More like sugar stimulates the fat cells – but hey, if I get to eat a couple of those yummy green frog cakes, a specialty of the *Flour and Icing* bakery, I'm all for it."

Loud voices, followed by a high-pitched baby laugh on the other side of the office door, broke into our conversation. Dana, arriving with baby Jake and three-year-old Kayla.

"Hope you haven't started without us." Dana pushed through the door with one hand while clasping a giggling Jake to her shoulder with the other.

Kayla, her little face serious, carefully made her way across the room and placed a large brown paper bag full of grapes on Nathan's desk. "These are for you and Abi," she told Nathan in her earnest little-girl voice. "My mum said grapes cool your blood."

Nathan raised one eyebrow at Dana and a smile tugged at his lips. "Did she now?"

Kayla sat down on the sofa next to me. She took my hand in her small one. "And we bought an apple for you, Aunty Molly."

"Why an apple?" I asked, checking Dana's bland expression over Kayla's head.

Kayla grinned, the space where she'd recently lost a baby tooth to the fairies, making her look super cute. "'Cos fruit makes you grow big and strong and Mummy said–"

"Okay, darlin', I get the picture."

Dana grinned at me as she lay Jake on the other end of the sofa, arranged a cushion behind his head and went fossicking in her oversized bag for a bottle. "Here, sweetie. Drink this. You can have your fruit later."

Jake took the bottle, lay back and within seconds of his first suck, his face relaxed into an air of bliss. He even stopped sucking momentarily to send a little baby smile up at me. Talk about a heart-breaker.

By the time the coffee was brewed, Dana had Jake asleep and Kayla sitting cross-legged on the floor surrounded by her pencils and coloring books. Then, satisfied her children were settled, she dragged a chair up to the desk and produced a pad and a red and white speckled biro from her bottomless shoulder-bag. "Okay," she said looking around to make sure we were all paying attention. "Onto our investigation. Have you come up with anything yet, Nathan?"

Nathan's fingers stopped clicking on the keyboard and he looked up. "Um…Harry Driscoll recently took out a big loan and second mortgage on the house. Looks like he's left his wife with a heap of debts."

"Poor Lizzie," I said thinking of her shocked face when I told her what I'd found in the back of their dog trailer. And now she'd probably lose her home as well as her husband. "Hudson said his father was a serial womanizer. Probably hocked the house to pay for his 'fancy' women."

"If his fancy women were all like the Mayoress, it's a wonder Harry didn't mortgage the house sooner. The idiot man was way out of his class."

"What I don't understand," Abi tilted her head to the side and furrowed her brow in concentration, "is what did these women see in Harry? I mean, if you can believe the grape vine, he's supposedly bedded not just your average everyday show competitor but also rich, powerful and beautiful women. But how? Okay, Harry was polite, a real gentleman, but also middle-class, blah looking, and as dull as a bag of toffees."

"Maybe he turned into Superman in bed," suggested Dana.

"And word got around?" I added with a smirk.

Nathan grinned at Abi. "If that's all it takes, maybe I should start wearing a cape."

Abi returned the grin. "Baby, you don't need a cape."

Dana rolled her eyes. "Can we please do away with the retina-burning visuals and get back to our investigation?"

After taking a sip of coffee, I placed the cup back on the table. Very gently. The cups were small, pretty, but fragile. I wondered how many of Nathan's clients were afraid to drink their coffee for fear of damaging the delicate cup. Maybe someone should advise him to buy a set of thick coffee mugs to serve his clients. Might make them relax and divulge more secrets. "What about the McInerny family? Hudson said there was bitter rivalry in and out of the show ring between Harry and the McInernys. Could one of them have killed Harry?"

Abi nodded. "Harry's dog, Scout, kept beating the McInerny's imported giant Schnauzer. That must have taken its toll on their import's stud duties, which would also mean a gaping hole in their bank account."

"Aha," said Nathan studying his computer screen. "Seems like the McInerny's twenty-year-old-son Jason, is a bit of a hot head. He's got form for second-degree aggravated assault. Spent three months in Mobilong prison last year for breaking a man's jaw in a fight over a packet of cigarettes."

"Sounds like a real sweetie." Abi shook her head. "But would he kill the owner of a dog just because it beat his father's dog in the show ring? That seems a bit far-fetched."

Dana shook her head. "I've actually spoken to Jason a few times at the shows and he's actually okay when he's on his own. It's when he meets up with those drunken mates of his that he becomes obnoxious."

"And wouldn't it be more effective in that scenario to kill the *dog*?" I said rubbing at the ache my temples. "With Harry dead, Lizzie will probably sell Scout onto another show competitor or she could get one of her sons to handle him at the shows for her. Which means the McInerny's expensive import will still get beaten."

Nathan frowned and jotted something down on the pad beside him. "Maybe he just isn't that smart."

Abi shivered. "Thank God for that. I've only had Scout in my care for a couple of days and he's already wormed his way into my heart. The dog's the innocent party in all this "

We lapsed into silence for a few minutes. Abi rubbed the goose bumps from her arms. Dana passed Kayla a small bunch of grapes before snaffling a vanilla square for herself and I thought of the monogrammed handkerchief we'd found beside the green litterbin in the park.

I leaned my elbows on the desk and looked around at my friends.

"When are we going to discuss what happened at Pettigrew Park?"

Dana sent me an eyeroll. "What happened is off-the-planet weird."

"And creepy," Abi added. "Who blackmails their own spouse?"

"Michael, evidently," reiterated Dana. "But even a bully like Michael wouldn't blackmail his wife if she *murdered* Harry."

Nathan glanced up from the keyboard. "Sounds more like he's making her pay for *sleeping* with Harry."

"You're right. If he thought Rhianna was a murderer, he'd go to the police. He's the Mayor. He has his reputation at stake."

"What a manipulating bug-eyed toad." Abi screwed up her nose. "Why couldn't he just accuse her of cheating and file for divorce. You know, like a normal ticked-off husband."

"Cause he's *not* normal," I said thinking back to the way he was bullying his wife while we were at their house that morning.

"If you ask me," Abi said frowning, "Rhianna needs to be told."

"You're right. Anyone who could blackmail his own wife could be dangerous. What if that's not the end of it? What if he has more weird stuff planned for her?"

"I agree," said Dana and grinned at me. "So, Molly, when are you going to tell her?"

"Hey, not me. No way. You missed out on the last trip to the Hamilton-Davies, so I'm nominating you as the bearer of weird news this time."

"We'll all go," said Abi with a grin. "In fact, I wouldn't trade watching Rhianna's reaction to this little newsflash for a lavish three-course meal at the Stamford Grand."

"I'll ring and make an appointment for us to see her tomorrow." Dana scribbled a note on her pad and then straightened her shoulders.

"All in agreement?"

I closed my eyes. Yes, Rhianna should be warned. Yes, it was the right and honourable thing to do. But was I looking forward to it? Ugh. I'd rather visit Monarto Zoo and have a picnic lunch with the lions.

12

"An astute handler always knows where the judge is standing in the show ring." Rhianna Hamilton-Davies, dressed in a smart navy designer suit over a white-and-navy-spotted bow- necked shirt, gazed earnestly at her audience from behind the microphone situated at the front of the dais. "This allows the handler to ensure the judge never sees her dog standing incorrectly and thereby revealing faults."

I fidgeted in my chair at the back of the crowded room. It was one of those uncomfortable generic plastic chairs bought or hired in batches of a hundred for all big functions. Being here today didn't make a lot of sense to me. How were we supposed to warn Rhianna that her husband was blackmailing her while a couple hundred people listened in? But according to Dana, the only time the oh-so-busy Mayoress/judge/social butterfly could fit us into her already overcrowded schedule was during a ten-minute break at the end of her lecture.

She'd already been talking for twenty minutes on what judges look for in a show dog – *'dogs are not necessarily judged against each other, but individually, as dogs that can carry on the best of their breed's characteristics to the next generation'*.

Hmm…did that mean Busta would pass on his mischief to the next generation if he sired a litter? I smiled as I pictured ten baby Bustas, all chasing fluffy cats and high-fiving each other whenever their quarry took refuge in a tree.

"The perfectly coiffed dog you see standing on the winner's dais at a big event might make showing look effortless to the spectator," Rhianna continued, her voice both knowledgeable and strong. "But it's always the consistent work performed away from the show ring that leads to best in breed, best in group, and finally best in show."

Now, in my mind, the ten baby Bustas were gaiting rhythmically around the show ring, all beautifully groomed and looking like winners. However, after two pups slammed on their brakes refusing to move, one broke loose from his handler and the cheekiest of all grabbed the judge's shoe in his mouth and bit a hole in the toe, I blocked the images and turned my thoughts to our coming conversation with Rhianna. I didn't even know how Dana had managed to talk the snooty show judge into giving up her ten-minute break to speak with us. All Dana would say was that the Mayoress owed her a favor. And didn't elaborate. Abi thought she'd probably dangled a free bath for her two miniature poodles, but I couldn't see that as an enticement. The judge was capable of bathing her own dogs and anyway, her two poodles were so tiny and delicate they'd likely get lost in Dana's hydro bath.

"Before I pass you on to other lecturers who have come here today to convey tips on grooming both short and long-haired dogs, I'd like to finish off with one last word of advice." Rhianna tipped her head to one side and put on her serious judge-face. "Confidence is a key trait found in all top show dogs. Confidence gives a dog the winning stride and attitude that judges love to see. But to attain this confidence your dog needs to be socialized from an early age. Take your puppies everywhere you go. Get them used to loud noises, people petting them and while they are still at the learning stage, let them meet and mingle with other dogs. That's the big secret to handling a dog who steps into the show ring, ignores everything around except his handler and says, 'Look at me! I'm the King of the World!"

After the enthusiastic clapping ceased and a tall thin man in his late fifties wearing thick glasses and a tweed jacket with leather inserts in the elbows replaced her on the dais, Abi, Dana and I scrambled to our feet and trailed Rhianna through the door of the conference room and out into the courtyard.

"Tell me again why you couldn't fill me in over the phone?" Rhianna, heels clicking on the cement, flounced across the courtyard to a covered nook. Not checking to see if we were following, she dug into her bra and fished out a packet of cigarettes.

"Because it's personal. This needs to be said face-to-face," Dana replied hurrying to catch up.

"Well, all I can say is it better be worth it." Rhianna lit a cigarette, leaned against the rough brick wall and inhaled deeply.

"Those things will kill you, you know," I told her moving out of range of the smoke.

"So will a bus if I'm so stressed I cross the road in a daze," she said removing the cigarette from her lips and watching the grey line of smoke drift skywards. After a few moments, she gave an exaggerated sigh before sending a stink-eye in our direction. "Okay, ladies, you've got me to yourselves. What's so important you need to intrude on the only free ten minutes I have in my day?"

Dana, never one to allow anyone to make her feel inferior, deflected the stink-eye with a snooty facade of her own. "Would the fact that we know the identity of your blackmailer, be worth that oh-so-valuable ten minutes?"

"B-blackmailer?" For a second the pretentious veneer slipped revealing raw vulnerability beneath. "What are you talking about?"

"The gray plastic bag stuffed with hundred dollar bills you left in the litterbin at the park?"

Rhianna glanced furtively left and right before rounding on Abi and me. "So, you two *did* come to my house to snoop," she snarled through gritted teeth. "I knew I shouldn't have left you alone in my office. Not only did you go through my desk drawers, if you found the blackmail note it means you leafed through my books." She paused, the air around her crackling and hissing with anger.

Put like that I felt like a slimy worm. "Sorry, but we were only investigating Harry's death."

"You say you know who's blackmailing me? How?" Rhianna visibly quashed her anger as she turned to Dana.

Whipping the white silk handkerchief from the back pocket of her jeans, Dana held the evidence up by two corners. "Recognize this?"

Rhianna's face paled. She snatched the handkerchief from Dana's hands and growled. Seriously, like a dog. "Where did you find this?"

"The blackmailer dropped it when he leaned off his scooter to extract the ransom money from the litterbin."

"*Michael.*"

One word with so much venom I almost expected the word to explode and die as it hit the air. For a moment I actually felt a little sorry for Michael Hamilton-Davies. But it only lasted a millisecond. Anyone perverted enough to blackmail their own spouse deserved every shred of vitriol thrown at them.

Dana nodded.

"Look, we're not here to make trouble." Abi leaned forward, the small frown between her eyes indicating concern. "We thought it best to warn you, that's all. We were worried your husband might have more abuse in store for you."

"Abuse?"

"Well, he's evidently punishing you for something. Already he's taken $100,000 of your money. Who knows what else he has planned?"

"Is he blackmailing you because you murdered Harry Driscoll?" I asked. Okay, it was no good pussy-footing around. We were investigating Harry's death, so if the blackmail money was for something unrelated, it wasn't any of our business.

Rhianna's laugh was so brittle it almost broke into shards as it bounced off the air. "Murdered? More like he found out I *slept* with Harry."

I blinked. Shook my head. I had to ask the question. Couldn't stand not knowing any longer. When Harry spoke to me in the Cafeteria, he reminded of the Mr. Cunningham, the father in *Happy Days*, not a sexy

Romeo, sought by every red-blooded woman on the show circuit.

"But why?" I said, completely lost. "What did Harry have that other men don't?"

"Oh, Moll, I don't think this is the time or place to…" Abi began.

"When I found the blackmail-note pushed under the front door, that's what I thought it was all about. Me sleeping with Harry," Rhianna broke in, completely ignoring my question. "Only reason I paid the money was so Michael wouldn't find out. And to think, it was that slimy puffed-up toad who left the note for me to find."

Rhianna tossed her half-smoked cigarette on the ground and stomped on it, so viciously, I figured, with each thrust and twist of her spiked high heel she was imagining her husband's face under the onslaught. "The Right Honorable Michael Hamilton-Davies, Mayor of Walkerton, won't know what hit him by the time I'm through with him. Every one of his dirty little secrets will be plastered out there for public viewing. Anonymously, of course. And I'll be there to soothe his wounded pride and fume at whoever is spreading the lies. And then, when he's at his lowest ebb, I'll slap a restraining order on him, file for divorce, and proceed to take that double-crossing rat to the cleaners."

Once again, I had a miniscule pang of compunction for Michael. When this woman was crossed, she turned into Godzilla's cranky sister.

Rhianna fished out a second cigarette and waved it in the air. "You know, if you're still investigating poor old Harry's death, I might have some useful information. Could be a bust of course, but either way, I don't want a breath of my name mentioned at any time. Right?"

"Our lips are zipped," said Dana. "Unless you're involved in his murder. Then all bets are off."

Rhianna's hackles rocketed, pulsating like a manic war dance. "How many times do I have to tell you, *I did not kill Harry*? He was my lover."

"Love can turn to hate," said Abi. "Especially when Harry had so many other notches on his bedpost. Did that bother you? Did you give Harry an ultimatum and he refused, so you stabbed him?"

Rhianna rolled her eyes and sighed, the fizz slowly seeping from her like a perished balloon. "God, you women are unbelievable. *One*, I said 'lover' not I 'loved' Harry. He was merely an incredible lay – end of story. And *two*, in case you missed the point, I am offering to help your investigation." She shook her head. "Now, do you want to know what I saw the day Harry was murdered, or not?"

I could see Rhianna was as close to a meltdown as a sibling of Godzilla could ever get so I reached out and squeezed her arm. "Of course, we do."

"Now, I'm not saying this means anything, and it's not because of what that rat of a soon-to-be-ex-husband did to me, but the day Harry was murdered I witnessed Michael and Harry having a ding-dong argument. Loud voices. Arms waving. The works. At the time, I suspected Michael had found out about Harry and my dalliance, so I kept well clear. But when I fronted Michael about it that night, he said Harry had let that over-friendly dog of his off the leash again and it had knocked a little girl over and licked her face. As a respected member of the community, he felt it was his duty to speak to Harry and warn him not to let it happen again."

She paused, head tilted to the side, before continuing. "Then, later in the day, looking very furtive and rather ridiculous in someone's old black hoodie with the hood pulled around his face, I saw Michael tailing Harry around the show-grounds. He even followed him into the cafeteria."

We all leaned closer, intent on every word. Animosity forgotten.

"And when I asked him why he was tailing Harry, he said he was merely ensuring the stupid little man didn't let his boisterous dog off the lead again." She paused again for effect. "Thing is, all this happened no more than an hour before Harry's body was discovered in his dog trailer."

Dana regarded the woman as if she had two heads. "And you didn't think to tell this to the police?"

"When you're constantly in the limelight like me, you tend to hide in the shadows whenever there's trouble. Plus, Michael is my husband.

I'm only passing this information onto you so you can, maybe, look into it on the quiet." She gave a nonchalant shrug of one shoulder. "Could be a clue. Or it could be exactly as Michael claimed. Okay, he's a bullying, manipulative, slimy snake, but I find it hard to see him as a murderer." She gave a half-snort. "Heaven forbid, he might get blood on his new Saint Laurent trousers."

I frowned at Rhianna. "There were two witnesses in the cafeteria who told the police someone followed Harry out the back entrance. One said it was a woman in red boots and the other said it was a guy in a hoodie." I frowned at Rhianna. "So, when you mentioned your red boots being stolen, we figured it was either you or the murderer stole your boots to frame you. But if it was Michael in the hoodie, that theory doesn't hold water."

She glanced down at her phone and rolled her eyes. "Ah, sorry, ladies, your ten minutes has expired. I'm due to open a fete in half an hour so I'll leave you to follow the clues – or whatever you do when you play at being detectives." Her lips curved upwards but the smile failed to reach her eyes. "And thank you for the tip-off. You can be sure Mr. Silk Handkerchief will be using cheap boxed-tissues in the not-too-distant future." She pushed herself off the wall and pitched another half-smoked cigarette onto the ground at her feet. "I suggest you three pop around and have a little chat with the *Honorable* Mayor. He's working from home today. Ask him a few down-to-the-bone questions. Twist his arm a little. See if you can get him to squeal like the pig he is."

I sighed. Easy for her to say. She'd be off prancing around at some gala opening, sipping champagne and shaking hands with other twittering celebrities, while we were off provoking a bully, a blackmailer and maybe even a murderer.

13

After Rhianna's revelation, Michael Hamilton-Davies shot to the top of our suspect list. There was opportunity – he'd been seen acting suspiciously while tailing Harry at the dog show and could easily have lured him to the trailer with the intent to kill. And he had motivation – Harry was bedding his wife. Being the controlling type, he probably decided that if Harry was out of the picture, Rhianna would be back under his thumb, and from there, back in his bed.

To be honest, I was all for going straight to the police with our evidence as tackling the Mayor on our own seemed equivalent to placing our heads in the lion's mouth. But as we'd promised Rhianna not to mention her name, I decided a chair and a long whip might come in handy.

After agreeing to meet at Abi's at 4.00pm to prepare ourselves for operation *Front the Mayor in his Den*, Abi took off for the *Pampered Pooch* to supervise their 25% off sale of doggy winter wear, Dana to *Hydro Hounds*, to ensure all dogs booked in for the afternoon metamorphized from the hydro bath shiny and smelling like flowers, and me to complete my word-count for the day.

Two hours later, I sat at my computer watching my favorite biro roll forward, then drop to the floor as Flerken, my cat, batted it off the desk with his right paw. Then, before the ever-watchful Busta could sink his teeth into the green and white plastic and carry the prize back to his bed, Flerken was onto it, tossing the pen in the air and catching it between his claws and teeth. A miniature tiger, with identical killer instincts, I could understand why mice never partied in my unit.

It was now 3.00pm and my word count for the day was barely at the quarter way mark. In fact, I'd been staring at a blinking curser for the last fifteen minutes. Couldn't get my mind away from the feel of Hudson's cool lips pressed against mine and back to solving the present dilemma between Tabitha and Gray in Chapter Seven.

They'd finally succumbed to their sexual urges but now Tabitha was disgusted with herself and telling Gray she never wanted to see him again. What was wrong with her? She was a slut. She'd jumped from one man's bed to another. No wonder Ethan left her at the altar. How could she be in love with Ethan and yet before the shock waves died down hop in bed with his best friend?

I let out a long breath, rolled my eyes and stared at the ceiling.

If Great Granny Teresa was still alive today, she'd faint if she read one of my hot romances. Books like, *'The Kama Sutra Love-In'* and *'Three in a Bed'*, both best-sellers, would have her reaching for the smelling salts.

Sometimes, I couldn't understand where it all came from myself. I'd been brought up so strictly, I was still a virgin, and yet when I sat down to write other people's love stories, I disappeared into another world. A world where wild urges and emotions that I'd never experienced in real life just came naturally to my characters.

After rescuing the green and white pen, very carefully, from Flerken's mouth, I trotted into the kitchen to stretch my legs and made another cup of coffee. Whenever I hit a blank wall in my writing, coffee and biscuits – especially chocolate Tim Tams – usually helped get me back on track.

Only today, the caffeine didn't seem to be working. This was the third cup of coffee and fourth chocolate Tim Tam – a salted caramel at that – and I still couldn't focus on my fictional characters. Hudson's real-life face as his lips met mine, soft and irresistible, kept intruding.

Maybe if I relaxed in the old beat-up armchair out on the patio, right away from my desk-top computer, sipped my coffee and let my mind explore that kiss a little further, I'd be in a better frame of mind to return to Tabitha's post-sex anguish.

What was it about Hudson that drew me to him like a moth to a flame? A guy who rode around on a Harley and dressed like a member of a biker gang was light years away from my ideal man. Although, even with his tats and piercings there was something about Hudson that screamed, *I'll take care of you and respect you.* But if I gave him my heart, would he disappoint like all the others? Would he demand sex without showing any love and then walk away when I refused?

Soft fur brushing against my left leg had me looking down to find Flerken with a second biro in his mouth and my watch declaring it was 3.45p.m.

I pinged to my feet. It couldn't be that late. My watch must be wrong. No way could I have been sitting outside for three-quarters of an hour thinking of Hudson.

I clicked on my phone which informed me my watch was spot on. It was now 3.46 p.m.

Oh. My. God.

As I rushed inside, the pleading eyes of the only man in my life I could really trust gazed up at me. I shook my head. "Sorry, Busta, you can't come."

I had fourteen minutes to find my shoes and jacket, put Busta outside and drive to Abi's house.

*****

I was five minutes late, but Dana was even later.

Her last client, a wayward boxer dog, quite a bit larger than the average boxer and according to Dana, on a diet of rump steak and weight-lifting steroids, had fought her for the entire wash. He'd scrambled to get out of the hydro bath, giving her a black eye and several nasty scratches in the process. So, by the time *Sweetums* marched down the ramp, coat shiny and smelling of rose petals and wearing a malevolent smirk like a badge of honor, Dana was drenched – right through to her bras and knickers – which necessitated a trip home and a complete change of clothes.

"Should have charged the owner double," she grumbled as she climbed into the back seat of Abi's van, buckled up and passed around a bag of licorice-all-sorts.

"Or given her a calling card with a phone number for the nearest Animal Behaviorist," I said turning around in my seat to select a licorice jube covered in green sprinkles and examine Dana's eye more closely. Seemed like the hard, bony head of a boxer dog and the soft flesh under the human eye didn't mix. She'd have a real shiner by morning.

Abi switched on the engine and backed out of her driveway. "So, what's the plan for when we arrive at the Hamilton-Davies?"

I shrugged. "I guess we knock on the door and when the Mayor opens it, ask him if he killed Harry."

Dana almost choked on her licorice. "Oh God, Molly, you are so naive. We can't just up and accuse him like that. We have to sweet-talk our way inside first."

"And *then* ask him if he killed Harry."

"No, no, no. We *question* him. Okay? No outright accusations. We ask him if he noticed anything suspicious on the day Harry was killed. You know, like if he saw anyone lurking near Harry's dog trailer – stuff like that. We're not the police, Moll. We're not going in there to arrest the man, just check if Rhianna's telling the truth. She could be dropping Michael right in it because she's so peed off after finding out he blackmailed her."

"What if he doesn't answer the door?" said Abi concentrating on the road as she drove toward the Hamilton-Davies' house. "All he has to do is peek through one of his front windows, see it's us, and then give us the finger."

"Mm…you're right, the guy's a snob and we're not blessed with double-barrel names, loaded, or high-up in society. We're merely commoners – lowly bugs he's inclined to stomp on or ignore," said Dana. "So, if he refuses to open the door, we might need to instigate plan B."

"Plan B? No one mentioned a plan B to me. What's plan B?" I was still trying to get my head around finding out if Michael murdered Harry without actually asking him.

"Let's see." Dana munched on her licorice-all-sort for a couple of minutes before continuing. "Molly, do you have your lock picks in your bag?"

Prickles ran up my spine and did the hokey-pokey in my chest. "I-I guess so." Because I kept losing my front door key, I'd bought a set of lock picks a few months back and learned how to use them via YouTube videos. I'd tested them out a couple of times on my own front door and they'd worked, but I didn't like the direction this conversation was heading.

"Good," said Dana. "How'd you like to try them out on a real lock? I know you've used them on that excuse for a front door at your place, but I'm expecting the security at the Hamilton-Davies to be quite a bit more state-of-the-art."

I turned and stared at her, my mouth open. Speechless.

"But that's breaking and entering." Abi sounded equally aghast. "You can't ask Molly to do that. She could end up in jail."

Which would not please my readers. Or me. I frowned at Dana. "That's your plan B? Me, breaking into the house?"

"Not exactly. I was thinking more along the lines of…" Dana's voice trickled off and came to an abrupt halt.

We'd turned into Jacaranda Avenue, the quiet affluent street shaded by purple foliage, only to discover it awash with police cars. They were parked on both sides of the road. An ambulance, lights flashing, squatted in the driveway of number 82, the Hamilton Davies' house, while uniforms and plain-clothes police milled around on the front lawn like ants at a picnic.

"Holy Catsfeet!" said Abi, her voice a croak. "What's going on here?"

Suddenly, I wasn't interested in learning about Dana's Plan B, I was too busy gaping at the live CSI show materializing in front of our eyes.

Something big was going down at number 82 and it didn't look good.

14

Disregarding the two uniformed policemen who were shouting and waving their arms in our direction, Abi maneuvered the van into the only parking space left on the curb. I tumbled out onto the footpath, so fast, one of my shoes skittered under Abi's van. I left it there. Too busy gaping at the poker-faced paramedics shouldering their way through the Hamilton-Davies' open front door.

One each end of a stretcher and one following behind.

Straightaway two harried policemen came scuttling across the lawn to inform us that we were violating a crime scene and to please leave the area immediately.

They may as well have been talking to the footpath.

Mesmerized, I watched as the paramedics progressed down the path toward the waiting ambulance. Why was the third paramedic trailing along behind instead of attending to the patient? Why were they moving so slowly? Surely whoever had been hurt needed to get to the hospital as soon as possible.

That's when I noticed the lights on top of the ambulance had stopped flashing, leaving a sudden deafening silence.

Goosebumps cantered up my arms.

Pulling my jacket around me to ward off the chill, I took a step closer for a better view and immediately gulped down a wad of horror. On the wheeled stretcher lay a body, completely covered by a sheet. Even the patient's face was hidden beneath the sheet.

Had the gardener made a fatal mistake with his pruning shears?

Had Michael decided to finish Rhianna off in a fit of rage?

Or was it the Mayor lying under that sheet? Had he paid the ultimate price for blackmailing his own wife?

"Can you see who it is?" Abi whispered in my ear, clearly as traumatized as me.

My throat too tight to speak, I shook my head.

"And we can't very well run over there and lift the sheet off his or her face to see who's underneath, can we?"

I shook my head again. More vigorously this time.

A woman, shouting obscenities, was escorted through the front doorway of the house, a policeman each side, her hands manacled behind her back, blood covering the front of her pink leisure suit.

Lady Hamilton-Davies...

I let out a quick sigh of relief. At least Rhianna, our demanding Mayoress wasn't under that white sheet. She might be a snob but she was a feisty snob and I sort of respected her spirit and fearlessness. But what had gone wrong? Her plan was to quietly and unobtrusively pay her husband back for blackmailing her – not kill him.

A middle-aged woman from the house next door, face covered in green gloop and wearing an ankle-length dressing gown leaned over the fence, all the better to get a better view of the proceedings.

"They were out the back in the courtyard, yelling and screaming," she told us. "I even heard crashing and thumping, as though they were throwing pot-plants at each other. My husband and I didn't know what to do, so in the end Gerald rang the police." She shook her towel-covered head, her eyes glued to the rear of the ambulance where the body on the stretcher was currently being lifted into the back. "But we didn't expect *this*."

One of the policemen who'd been hustling us to get back in our car and drive away from the crime scene gave a shout and pointed at a News van angling around the corner of the street. Immediately, six uniforms raced toward the van ready to intercept.

How did the Media hear of this so quickly? Who tipped them off? Maybe they trained pigeons to keep a look out for anything newsworthy and report the scoop back to their newsroom. As the vehicle came to a halt and two journalists and a photographer began to open their doors, the police went into lockdown mode, threatening anyone who took a photo of the crime scene with instant arrest.

Guess dead Mayors have more rights than us ordinary mortals.

While the police argued with the reporters, Abi, Dana and I checked the action transpiring on the Hamilton-Davies' front lawn – where Rhianna, despite her handcuffs, was busy kneeing one of her jailers in what appeared to be a very sensitive part of his anatomy.

"I didn't kill Michael," she yelled and if she'd been a dog the hairs along her back would be bristling and her teeth gnashing together in a snarl. "Take these handcuffs off me so I can go after the bastard who did."

She looked up, spotted Dana – we still didn't know what favor she owed Dana – and her face lit up in recognition. Then, while the second policeman jostled Rhianna in the direction of the waiting squad car, she called out. "Dana, I'm innocent and I want to engage your *Chicks* to investigate Michael's death."

Dana started towards Rhianna but met a brick wall dressed as a policeman. She continued the conversation over his left shoulder. "What happened?"

"Okay, Michael and I argued, but then I went inside to change out of my work clothes – and to get away before I got any angrier and blew my plan by accusing him of blackmailing me." She grabbed another breath to steady herself. "I was only gone ten minutes and when I came back out onto the patio, he was…he was just lying there…in a pool of blood." Her face seemed to fall in on itself momentarily and her voice petered out as though reliving the image in her head. She visibly pulled herself together before continuing. "Yes, I intended to divorce Michael – but I would never kill him."

"What about the blood on your clothes?"

She looked down at the large splotch of blood on her clothes as though just becoming aware of it. "Guess I got that when I tried to resuscitate him – but he was already dead."

The second policeman, red in the face and walking like a constipated duck joined his friend to help open the back door of the police car and assist their captive into the back seat.

"Okay, Rhianna, we're on it," Dana assured her before the car door closed with a resounding finality. "When you arrive at the station, ring your lawyer, and then leave the investigation to us."

"To us?" I repeated, frowning.

"Why not? I bet Michael and Harry's killer are one and the same person," said Abi. "All we have to do is find out who murdered Harry and we're home free."

I hated to disillusion my two eager-beaver *Chicks*, however, it had to be said. "Are you forgetting we thought Michael murdered Harry."

"Yes, there is that." Dana nodded her head as the police car carrying a scowling Mayoress – or would that be ex-Mayoress now her husband was dead – out of the driveway and in the direction of the police station. "So, it looks like we're back to square one."

Further back than square one…

The Honorable Michael Hamilton-Davies had been our only valid suspect. The only suspect who'd ticked all our boxes.

Now every box was empty.

*****

"What now?" Abi's hands shook on the steering wheel as she drove away from Jacaranda Avenue. Once Detective Lightfoot arrived at the scene, he'd quickly herded us back into Abi's van, warning if he could still see the van's number plate when he finished counting to ten, he'd book us for obstruction. That's after he ordered one of the policemen who'd been attempting to shift us earlier to crawl under the car and relocate my lost shoe.

I actually felt a small tinge of respect for this guy who had the steely glare thing down pat and although Dana promised Rhianna that we'd find Michael's killer, I figured with Detective Lightfoot on the case, maybe we weren't alone.

"D'ya think *she* did it?" I asked, not ready to completely rule the woman out yet, especially knowing how her temper was as easily triggered as her now-dead husband's. I gave a one-shouldered shrug. "Look at it this way – with Michael dead, she won't have to share the house and money with him, or pay a fortune to engage a top divorce lawyer."

"Come on, Molly," said Dana. "You saw her. She's devasted. She was reaching out to us for help because she's afraid she won't get justice from the court system."

"What about the blood on her clothes?"

"She explained that. She was giving Michael mouth to mouth in a vain attempt to get him breathing again."

"Maybe she did it," put in Abi changing lanes to pass a slow-moving truck, "but she's not high on my list."

I shook my head. "Well, if it wasn't Rhianna, it means the killer strolled into the courtyard while she was inside changing, quietly disposed of Michael, then calmly sauntered out through the front gate, climbed into his car and drove off. All without anyone in the street seeing him. Yet their next-door neighbors, who were listening in on their argument and called the police, didn't see or hear anyone go in or out of the house. Sounds a bit off to me."

"What if he was already there? He could have been lurking behind some shrubbery waiting to catch Michael alone, then, when he'd finished the job, snuck over the back fence."

I let out a frustrated sigh. Dana's theory was a likely scenario, but to clear Rhianna of the murder charge, how were we supposed to investigate this line of thinking? With the police crawling all over the Hamilton-Davies' property, there was no way we could break in and hunt for clues.

Break in and hunt for clues?

That's when a chilly knot threaded itself around most of the important organs inside my chest and tightened as the reality thumped me in the gut.

Why on earth would we want to go looking for clues to his identity? This monster had already killed twice – what's to say he wouldn't kill again?

15

By the time I arrived home, brain leaking fear, confidence at a low ebb, the only two things keeping me from crawling into bed, dragging the quilt over my head and staying put for a week, were my two fur-babies, Busta and Flerken.

I could hear Busta's high-pitched, *Yay! Mum's home!* bark from the backyard as I pulled into the driveway, and my odd-ball cat, who must have been hunkered down waiting on the small oak table near the front door, listening to my footsteps on the gravel as I walked from the car, launched himself from the table into my arms and then decided to wrap his body around my neck, like a scarf. I cuddled him to me as I hurried through the kitchen to let Busta inside.

I loved these two guys. From his perch on my shoulders, Flerken's rough tongue rasped against my cheek, while Busta, his face one huge delighted smile, bounced and twirled and barked, then rubbed his whole body up against me. It's hard to explain, but the touch of their velvety fur as it caressed my skin somehow drove out the bad vibes, giving me hope and a boost to my confidence.

After filling their food bowls with dry kibble and batting away the unkind thought that maybe food had been the driving force behind all that display of love and devotion, I made myself a coffee and sat at the kitchen table to write down a list of suspects. With Michael's untimely death, the list had grown shorter.

Rhianna – has a volatile temper/ was addicted to whatever skills Harry brought to the bedroom/ her husband was blackmailing her/ she had a legitimate reason to kill her husband.

Hudson – I didn't want to add his name to the list but he *did* have a motive. Hudson hated the cavalier way his father cheated on his mother. But why murder the Mayor?

Lizzie Driscoll – the cuckolded wife who had opportunity – she was sitting within a hundred feet of the dog trailer. Like Hudson, she had a motive to kill her husband, but what reason would she have to murder the Mayor?

A member of the McInerny family – after paying a huge price for their imported Schnauzer, Harry's dog, Scout, kept beating their dog in the show ring. Consequently, the fall in stud fees was sending the McInernys bankrupt. But once again, why kill Michael?

I chewed on my bottom lip as I dug deep for inspiration. Every suspect on my list had a motive for killing Harry, but, except for Rhianna, none had a motive for doing away with Michael. There was no connection.

Or was there?

What if the greedy manipulative Mayor was not only blackmailing his wife, but also the murderer? What if, when he was tailing Harry at the show, suspecting him of having it off with his wife, he witnessed whoever stabbed Harry with the dog-grooming scissors, in the act? Hmm…I'd say that was an excellent motive to smash the blackmailer's head in with the sharp edge of a shovel.

Okay, I may not be as tough as Dana, or have the bubbly confidence exuded by Abi, but I figured my creative writer's brain might prove useful to the *Gumshoe Chicks* after all.

Feeling a little smug, I slid my phone from my pocket and prepared to text my friends, find out what the *Chicks* thought of my latest theory. If the Mayor *had* blackmailed the murderer, the suspects for Harry's murder were the same suspects as for the Mayor's.

Before I could tap out the first text, there was a thunderous knock on my front door. Busta, ever alert, scuttled across the room, loudly informing the door-knocker that he was a fierce Rottweiler with a medal of honor from the Guard Dogs of Australia and to get past him they'd need protective armor. I wasn't expecting a caller, so, with a murderer on the loose, I glued my right eye to the peep-hole. It was a delivery guy, his digital gizmo held out to be signed and a square parcel tucked under his left arm.

"Sign here please," he said shoving his gizmo into my face the moment I opened the door.

"You sure it's for me? I'm not expecting a parcel."

"I just deliver 'em, lady, I don't send 'em." He shrugged, then glanced down at the grinning, tail-wagging fox terrier at my feet. "Cute pup."

"Yeah." I shook my head at the 'cute pup'. "Mind he doesn't bite your leg off at the hip if you move too quickly."

The delivery guy rolled his eyes.

After using my finger to create a weird distortion of my signature – *who can write with their finger on those things?* – I accepted the box and carried it inside.

"I didn't order anything online," I told Flerken who'd jumped up on the table to nose at the box, equally as interested in the contents as me. Busta, not happy to be out of the picture, hitched his front legs onto a chair and skated his head onto the table, all the better to see what was going down. "*And* it's not my birthday."

I checked the box-shaped parcel for the sender's name: Geraldine Green. Never heard of her. Maybe she was a fan of my books.

I tore at the wrapping paper, candy pink, and dropped the sheets on the floor for Busta to play with. He was more interested in whatever was inside the box. His whines urging me to unwrap faster.

"Now we have to dig through all this shredded paper," I told my two interested spectators after lifting the lid of the large box and diving inside. "There's enough shredded paper in here to bed a horse."

My curiosity aroused, I tunneled through the paper, casting it on the floor in my haste, until I came across another box. A flat black box with a pretty silver star-spangled lid.

Intriguing.

Flerken attempted to bury his head inside the parcel, while Busta's whining upped several decibels.

"Hey, guys, give me a bit of elbow room here. The parcel's addressed to me, not you, so it's unlikely to be a box of gourmet dog or cat treats."

They weren't convinced.

Gently removing Flerken's head and front paws from inside the parcel for the third time, I lifted the black box out and placed it carefully on the table.

I stared at it for a moment, slightly uneasy, as though expecting a jack-in-the box to suddenly jump up and scare me out of my panties.

Flerken however was completely untroubled. With Busta egging him on, he flicked at the lid with his paw, knocking it part-way off. It didn't explode and I didn't turn into a frog, so I reached out and lifted the lid the rest of the way off.

And did a double-take.

A copy of *Kama Sutra Love-In*, my latest romance novel, published only a month ago, stared back at me.

What the heck?

Confused, I gazed at the cover where my two love interests, Rebecca and Sebastian, stood, arms wrapped around each other, locked in a kiss. The kissing, however, was proving difficult because someone – whoever had sent the parcel – had carefully cut off Rebecca's head.

Immediately, the chicken and salad sandwich I'd eaten for lunch threatened to make a messy re-appearance.

What did this mean?

Who'd decided to behead my fictional heroine and send me the result of his crazed scissor attack?

And why?

I spotted a pretty powder-pink envelope half-hidden beneath the book. Hoping it might give me some answers, I slid the envelope out, lifted the flap and removed a greeting card from inside. Immediately, my breath caught in my throat and I began to shiver. It wasn't a 'Get Well' card – or a 'Wish you were here' card – or even a belated Valentine's Day card. Nope. This insidious Hallmark message featured a photo of me on the front, sitting at my desk, barefoot, wearing my daggiest sweat pants and a sloppy *Love Me Love My Dog* tee. Flerken was curled up asleep on the desk beside my computer and Busta, with his distinctive half-smile, sprawled diagonally across my bare feet…

A frisson of foreboding slithered up my spine as I realized this photo had been taken yesterday. I'd been sitting at my computer, working away on my current manuscript, completely oblivious to the fact that some creepy peeping-tom had a camera trained on me.

Why? How? To snap this photo, the perp must have been standing outside my window, looking in.

Mouth dry, I slowly opened the card, fear giving me three thumbs, slippery fingers and blurred vision as I attempted to focus on the chilling words printed in bold black type on the card inside.

'SEE HOW EASILY I CAN GET TO YOU?'

16

I sat on the floor in the kitchen, legs stuck out in front of me, back hard up against the refrigerator door, the pavers cold against the back of my legs. Busta, his soft brown eyes focused on me, lay his head on my lap, while Flerken once again jumped up and curled around my neck. In my head, I could picture the murderer skulking around outside my office window, a smirk on his face as he watched me tussle with my protagonists' romantic conflicts, imagined him running his eyes over me like a piece of meat before lifting his camera to record the scene.

All the while, my fingers absently smoothed Busta's fur, the texture and warmth comforting me, helping to settle my nerves.

And then the phone rang.

I jerked, heart-beat whipping up to macro-speed again. What if it was the murderer on the phone? What if he was ringing from somewhere up in the branches of the tree directly across the road, a rifle in one hand, a pair of binoculars in the other and a high-powered camera hooked on a strap around his neck?

It was Dana.

"You get a present too?" Her voice was so beyond angry it was almost a hiss.

I nodded. Then realized we weren't on Zoom or Skype, so she couldn't see me. Lips dry, I found I had to lick them before I could get the word out. "Yes."

"Know what he sent me?" She growled and not waiting for an answer barreled on like an out-of-control truck on a downward slope. "He sent me a disc with a complete record of all my *Hydro Hound* clients. Personal details. Bank account numbers. The lot."

"Oh, my God, how'd he get hold of that?"

"Mongrel's either been inside my house or he's gotten remote access to my computer."

"What are you going to do?"

I could hear her sigh filter through the phone. "First I have to contact my clients so they can take precautions, then I'll bump up security on my computer and ring a locksmith to change the locks on our doors."

I told her about Rebecca's hacked-off head and the threatening words inside the card.

She said her message carried an identical warning.

"What about Abi?" I carefully unlatched one of Flerken's claws from the side of my neck without disturbing him.

"Abi's parcel was delivered to *Pampered Pooch*. Her box was full of dogs' turds and there was a photo of her with a pooper scooper, picking up after one of her customer's dogs."

"And she doesn't know who took the photo?"

"Not a clue."

This was like a bad dream, only worse – it was real. "So…wh-what are we going to do?"

"Thumb our noses at the perp, of course. Show him he doesn't scare us."

"B-but he does! Scare us, that is." I tried to swallow but the lump in my throat was too dry. "Shouldn't we back off? Stop asking questions so he'll leave us alone? Won't what you're suggesting put us in more danger?"

"Molly, you can't trust a murderer. If we back off the investigation now, that leaves him out there to kill again and we'll still be shaking in our boots whenever we're at home alone or walking in the street after dark. Do you want to be constantly peering over your shoulder?

Worrying whether he'll break into the house to take more intrusive photos – or worse – just to prove he can?"

Dana was right. There'd be no peace until this monster was caught and put away. Not that it made standing up to him any easier. I blew out a sigh of frustration. "But why us? Why can't we just leave the investigation to the police?"

"We're in too deep now, Moll, plus we also have Rhianna soliciting our help."

"But–"

"Hey, we're the *Gumshoe Chicks*. We have a reputation to uphold." She growled deep in her throat again. "Plus, I want to personally kick this pervert's butt."

Busta, evidently sensing my misery, reached up and licked my cheek, then sprinted across to his toy box, selected his favorite Pooh Bear toy and deposited the battered lump of eyeless brown fur in the middle of my lap.

I pulled him closer and kissed the top of his head. "You're right, I guess. We can't relax until he or she is behind bars."

"And that's where we're going to put him." Dana's voice was no less angry, in fact it was white hot. "Meanwhile, I have Peter, Nathan is moving in with Abi, and we'll go to the police, show them our *presents* and insist Detective Lightfoot install a police car out the front of your house at night. Just until the murderer is caught. Right?"

I sniffed. "Right."

"Meanwhile, we ramp up our investigation, get out there, hunt for clues, interrogate suspects and root out this *creature*. Only way we'll be safe."

With Dana's compelling words ringing in my ears, I took a deep breath and let it out slowly. Okay, there were three of us – five if we included Dana's husband, Peter, and Nathan – and only one killer. He'd gone down a slippery path when he decided to threaten us, move into our personal space.

But we had to be vigilant.

Dana's voice interrupted my thoughts. "You still there, Moll?"

I gave a strangled laugh. "You know, if our amateur photographer was aiming his camera through my window right now, he'd find me flaked out on the floor, a cat wrapped around my neck, a smelly chewed-up Pooh bear on my lap and a concerned dog attempting to scramble into my arms."

"You'll be okay, Moll. But it's time to disband your team of furry allies – maybe suggest a shared tin of gourmet chicken, that'll work for all but the stuffed bear – gather together every shred of evidence, including torn paper and cardboard as well as what was inside the box and meet us outside the police station in an hour."

*****

Detective Lightfoot's exasperated eyeroll when he clocked us charging through the precinct doors an hour later, did not bode well for his cooperation.

Dressed in a nifty silver-gray suit with matching tie and spit polished black shoes, he could have been mistaken for the CEO of a highly successful company instead of a policeman.

"Detective!" Abi called out as he spun on his heel and made a dash for the safety of his office. "Stop! We need to talk to you!"

Arms overflowing with shredded paper and cardboard, Abi chased him down before he could disappear through his office door, but due to her limited view, she tripped, almost taking him out as her arms flailed and wrapping paper and dog turds flew high in the air.

"What the–" His shocked face, as an oozing turd landed with a squelch across the toe of his shiny black shoe turned to horror as Abi's outstretched fingers hooked onto the front of his trousers to keep herself erect.

It was like watching an imminent disaster while buried up to your neck in the sand.

"Um…sorry about that." An embarrassed giggle that sounded more like a chook's cluck escaped her lips, as red-faced, she righted herself, patted his trouser fronts down as though to smooth things back into place and stepped away. "Better not clean that off your shoe just yet though. It's evidence from a crime we're here to report."

Mouth open, he backed away through the doorway into his office and scuttled crablike behind his desk, as though the only thing in the Universe that mattered at that moment in time was to put three feet of solid oak between him and Abi's hands. Then, after waving us to the chairs on the opposite side of his desk he sat and dragged a laptop and a towering pile of official folders, more barriers, in front of him. "Er…right…now what can I do for you, ladies?"

No one answered. We couldn't. Abi's face was bright red, Dana's lips were sucked in as though holding back a flood of giggles and if my chest grew any tighter from holding onto the bubble of laughter, I'd burst. Finally, I grabbed a quick breath, counted to ten and thought of all the starving children in the world. Even then, it took all my control to respond without spitting out a giggle. "We have a crime to report."

"We're being stalked by Harry's murderer," said Abi staring at a spot on the wall at least four foot above the detective's head.

Dana slowly let the tortured air hiss from her lips and caught a new breath. She sat up straighter in her chair. "Plus, he sent each of us a threatening parcel. Everything's here for you to examine."

Detective Lightfoot eyed the array of torn wrapping paper, shredded paper, cardboard, black boxes and photos we'd shrugged off onto his desk and his nose gave an imperceptible nose-lift. Although Abi's little black box was now empty – the contents still on the detective's shoe – the smell was lingering.

"Take a look at this. He's been stalking us, taking photos of us in situations that means he had to be trespassing at the time." I slid the photo of me in my office working on my computer across the desk to him.

"And he's threatening us, trying to scare us away from the investigation." Abi flipped the card open to where the red-inked words, 'SEE HOW EASILY I CAN GET TO YOU', once again sent chills spiraling in my chest. "Couldn't get much creepier than that."

"Hmm…" At first, convincing the detective this was a genuine crime was like persuading a plump turkey that he'd have fun at a Thanksgiving dinner. However, by the time we'd finished our statements and he'd studied the evidence littering his desk, we had his full attention. He asked the right questions, passed every scrap of evidence on to forensics, including the scrapings off his left shoe, and promised to arrange for a patrol car to park outside my house at night.

And then he buzzed for two burly constables to escort us from his office to the front door and to make doubly sure we vacated the building.

Relieved to be away from the musty smell of incarceration – and poop – we waved the unsmiling uniforms goodbye and followed our noses around the corner to a little coffee shop, 'The Sea Urchin', where mouth-watering smells of aromatic coffee and newly baked pastries drew us like parched explorers to an oasis.

I loved this coffee shop. It maintained a traditional harbor theme with fishing nets, ancient wooden anchors and framed pictures of bygone boats adorning two walls while an aquarium displaying fish of every color lined the entire back wall.

Coffee, cakes and character – exactly what we needed to recuperate.

After checking my watch – it was close to 6pm and the sky was starting to darken – I squeezed into a little alcove at the rear of the shop with the other two Chicks, cappuccinos, three varieties of cake and several cookies spread out on a large plate shaped like a boat's steering wheel, in the center of the table. With one accord we decided to eat first, talk second.

After inhaling two choc-chip cookies, Abi licked a crumb from her lips and paused. "These are almost as yummy as the cookies Chi bakes."

"Mmm…except these aren't laced with marijuana." I bit into my second macadamia cookie and grinned at Abi. When we'd last visited Chi and his poodle-breeding partner Stephen, Abi had unintentionally eaten the cookies Chi baked especially for his retired poodles, with entertaining results. They'd been laced with hash to alleviate the old dogs' aches and pain.

"Okay," said Dana after finishing her first cup of coffee and ordering a second. "Enough of the cookie appreciation. Time to plan our next move. Whoever killed Harry knows we're poking around, so our next step is to push on and find out which of our suspects has a motive for also killing Michael."

"The only one with a motive for both is Rhianna," said Abi. "But it can't be her because she was in custody when our parcels arrived."

"Could have arranged for them to be sent before she was arrested," I said.

Dana snorted. "Can you *really* imagine our illustrious Mayoress sneaking around in her Gucci stilettos, camera slung around her neck, peeping through windows and shunting dog poo into a box to send through the mail?" She gave a snort. "I don't think so."

I suddenly remembering my earlier theory. "Actually, every one of Harry's suspects could have a motive for killing the Mayor."

Abi hitched one eyebrow while Dana took a sip of her coffee and studied me over the brim of her cup.

I went on in my best Nancy Drew voice. "What if Michael became greedy? What if, as well as blackmailing his wife for sleeping with Harry, he decided to enrich his bank account further by blackmailing Harry's killer?"

Dana's stare intensified. "But how would he know?"

"What if, when he was trailing Harry at the show, he took a photo – or better-still, a video – of the killer, in the act?"

Dana put her cup down and instigated a knuckle bump. "Good thinking, Ninety-Nine."

I smirked back at her. "And if the perp didn't come up with the dosh, old Michael would threaten to upload the video from his phone onto Facebook and ensure it went viral."

"So how do we get hold of the Mayor's phone?"

"We don't." said Dana with finality. "If what we're supposing was on Michael's phone, there's no way his killer would have left the evidence in his victim's pocket. The phone's more than likely swimming with the fishes in some out of the way river or creek by now. Or smashed into a trillion pieces and buried under a pile of garbage in a dumpster."

"You know," said Abi snagging the last cookie crumb on the plate with a dampened finger. "If I had something as vital as that on *my* phone, I'd definitely make a copy and hide it somewhere in my house. Wouldn't you?"

I nodded, not quite believing what I was about to propose. "And if you're suggesting what I *think* you're suggesting, I have a set of perfectly good lockpicks at home capable of opening the Hamilton-Davies' back door."

17

The sky was already sliding toward darkness as I turned into my driveway an hour later. *The Messenger*, a locally delivered newspaper lay sprawled in the middle of my miniscule front lawn, Busta's excited, here's-my-mum bark, a sound that always sent me gooey inside erupted from inside the house, and a solitary police car with a lone constable at the wheel squatted like a sentry no more than two feet from my letterbox.

Detective Lightfoot had followed up on his promise.

Immediately, conflicting thoughts crashed around in my head. Although a police presence was welcome, it also made sneaking out to visit the Hamilton-Davies' house later tonight a little trickier. A little more complex.

I pressed the remote on my keyring and watched the carport roller-door rise. Mind still on tonight's break-and-enter, I drove through and parked inside. We hadn't expected Detective Lightfoot to cooperate so quickly. If at all. Which meant our plans needed a slight tweak. I rummaged in my bag, snaffled my phone and texted both Dana and Abi, advising them not to pick me up from the front of my unit but in the next street, beside the public phone box.

My mind continued clocking through the details. With a policeman out the front, I'd now have to leave via the back door and climb over the other unit fences to reach our new meeting place. Hopefully this policeman didn't intend to knock on my door every couple of hours to check on me.

New plans sorted, I decided I'd better do the courteous thing and report to said policeman. Say hello. Thank him for his presence. Arrange a signal if I was in trouble and needed him in a hurry.

After pulling down the roller door I trekked across the lawn and tapped on his car window. "Good evening officer," I said and waited for him to lift his head from the paper work he was attending to. "Thanks for coming. If there's anything you need, just honk your horn." I peered into the darkened car, noting a large thermos and an unopened packet of chocolate TimTam biscuits nestled on the seat beside him.

The constable gave an involuntary jerk and looked up from his paperwork. His eyes, blue and familiar, widened, as though caught in a car's headlights.

"Hudson?" I blinked, leaned closer, unable to believe my eyes. Was I hallucinating? How could Hudson Driscoll, dressed in a police uniform, be parked in a police car outside my house? Hudson was a badass biker guy.

A panicked expression, laced with guilt, flashed across his face. "Molly, I can explain." Dropping a cluster of papers in his haste, he shoved the paperwork into the glovebox, yanked the car door open and scrambled onto the footpath.

"Explain? Explain why you didn't tell me you were a cop?" I let out an incredulous snort. "Now that should make the story of the year."

"I wanted to tell you, but…I don't know…the longer I left it the harder it became."

Anger bubbled in my chest at the thought of Hudson's deception. "Why? Because when you came to my house that night, you believed I murdered your father? Because you were sent there by the police, to coerce a confession out of me?"

"No, no, you've got it all wrong, Molly. The police didn't send me." He took off his police cap and ran a hand over the top of his head. I could see the long blonde hair, normally in messy waves and past his shoulders, was now tied back in a ponytail. The nose rings had disappeared and he was cleanly shaven. "I was only transferred from Salisbury to the Port Adelaide police station a week ago and was off duty when Dad was murdered. I raced home but Mum was almost comatose and I couldn't get any information from the station. Being so close, they wouldn't let me in on the case." He let out a ragged sigh. "Molly, I was out of my head with grief when I knocked on your door. All I knew for a fact was that you found Dad's body and at that time were a suspect. I just wanted to see you, talk to you. If you'd known I was a cop, you would have clammed up."

"So, you dressed up as a biker to get me confessing?" I shook my head, torn between punching him on the arm and bursting into tears.

"Molly, I *am* a biker. I'm a member of the Port Adelaide Biker's Club. And when the news of Dad's death came through, I was miles away, giving a lecture on motor bike maintenance at an Adult college."

Okay, maybe I wouldn't punch him – *yet*.

"But when you knocked on my door, you believed I'd killed your father?"

"Maybe…at first…but–"

"How could you imagine that of me?"

"I didn't know you then, Molly I–"

"And later, at the park – what about then?"

"By then I–"

"And outside Nathan's office when you…" The fire in my belly fizzled and turned to ashes. I couldn't go on.

"Molly," his voice softened and he placed a hand on my shoulder. I pulled away, stepped out of his reach. "It only took five minutes in your presence to realize what sort of person you were. That there's no way you were responsible for Dad's death. And as for our connection in the park and what happened between us outside your friend Nathan's office–"

"Don't say it." I recoiled even further. "You used me, Hudson. How can we possibly go on from that?"

Tears spiked at the back of my eyes. I blinked them away and sniffed. When Hudson kissed me and there was a connection, I'd actually allowed my guard down for the first time. Ever. Thought maybe there was something special between us to explore.

But he'd used me. Just like Ethan in my work-in-progress, when he left Tabitha at the altar because he'd been afraid to commit so changed his mind. Who does that? Professes to love someone, proposes, and then shrugs his shoulders and walks away before the minister can finish saying, 'Do you take this woman for your beloved wife?' Shit-for-brains lying Ethan – that's who.

Biting down on my bottom lip, I dragged in a scratchy breath.

And now, when I'd finally stepped away from my fictional romance-book lovers and believed that maybe I'd found the one guy in real life I could trust – I discover he'd used me too.

As I stood lasering a death-stare at Hudson, who, if I was honest, actually looked even cuter in a police uniform than the black leather-look, the suspect list I'd compiled only that morning, while sitting at my kitchen table, flashed across my mind. Wasn't Hudson's name on my list? And when he'd knocked on my door that first night, didn't I think he could be the murderer? And after he'd confided in me that he hated the way his dad treated his mother, hadn't I suspected Hudson of killing his father to protect his mother?

I let out a sigh and gazed up into those deep blue eyes regarding me from under the police cap. Eyes the color of the sea on a bright sunny day. Eyes full of pain, as he struggled to get his message across.

We were at a cross-road.

I reached out, took his hand and squeezed. Hudson had lost his father in the worst possible way. Okay, he'd come looking to me for answers, not fully revealing who he was, but wouldn't I have done the same thing in his shoes? I moved closer. "I'm sorry, it's just a lot for me to process, suddenly seeing you here, and finding out you're actually not a badass biker after all."

He lifted one eyebrow and grinned. "A badass biker, eh? Hmm…I like that. In fact, when we go for a burn on my Hog, tomorrow, I might even let you check out my badass tattoo."

"I look forward to it."

He moved away slightly, straightened his cap and I smiled as the muscles under his uniform rippled. "However, tonight I'm here on official police business. Detective Lightfoot assigned me to keep a watch on your house, instruct you to stay inside, lock your doors and if there's the slightest noise, contact me. Either ring me – you have my number – or if you can't get to the phone flash the lights on and off twice. Okay?"

I nodded, barely able to stop myself from blurting out what we *Chicks* had planned for tonight. Here he was being all protective and caring while I was planning to sneak out the back way and deliberately put myself in danger.

"I heard about the photos and the threats. You must be scared out of your wits. But don't worry, Molly, I won't move from this spot until nine tomorrow morning. Okay?"

I nodded again, tightening my fingers around my bag as I turned to walk up the path to the front door of my unit.

"No-one, and I mean *no-one*, will get to you, Molly. Not while I'm on patrol. Don't forget – if you need me, flash your lights on and off twice, and I'll come running."

Me and my big mouth.

I turned the key in the front door, battled my way past Busta and Flerken and tossed my bag on the kitchen table. Why had I offered to test my lockpicks on the Hamilton-Davies' back door tonight? Tonight, of all nights. And there was no way I could confide in Hudson – not now I knew he was a cop. Which meant I had to go behind his back, sneak out of the house while he was doing his duty protecting me. And what if Detective Lightfoot found out and Hudson lost his job through my duplicity?

I ran tight fingers through my already messed up hair. And what if, after all this, Hudson decided I was too flaky – that was the word he'd used to describe me on that first night – and withdrew the offer for another ride on his Hog and a view of his badass tattoo?

I couldn't do it. Couldn't risk losing this chance with Hudson. As I snatched up my phone, ready to cancel tonight's event, I caught sight of Busta's bright perky brown and white face, chocolate eyes twinkling, ears pointed like two starched tents. He'd raided his toy box, and once again pooh bear hung out of his mouth. One front paw on my leg, he offered his favorite bedraggled lump of fur to me.

I dropped my phone back in my bag and let out a couple of heartfelt curses. Cancelling wasn't an option. Both Busta and Flerken starred in the photo taken by the murderer, while Penelope was prominent in Dana's and Chloe in Abi's.

Coincidence? Not likely.

So, even if there was only a one percent chance of finding evidence in the Hamilton-Davies' home, we had to take it.

And if Hudson didn't understand my motives, he wasn't the right man for me.

Once Busta's nose was deep in a bowl of gourmet free-range chicken and Flerken was tucking into choice Albacore sea-salted tuna, I tossed a box of Mac and Cheese into the microwave and set the table for one. One plate, one fork, one serviette, pepper shaker and an economy-sized bottle of ketchup.

Three hours to fill before I met up with Abi and Dana outside the phone box in the next street. My whole body twitched as I finished my meal, scraped off the excess sauce and cheese, slotted my fork and plate into the dish washer. Too uptight to concentrate on writing, I had to keep active – pacing, cleaning, rearranging – or I might chicken out completely.

After vacuuming every room and scouring the grout between the tiles in the bathroom, I polished my lockpicks until I could see my pale face in the shine, then dragged all my clothes from the large wardrobe in my bedroom, hunting for the perfect break-and-enter outfit. After all, this could be the outfit I wore to prison if we were caught. Should I get decked out in something colorful and flamboyant to keep me charged up and motivated, or dress head to toe in black to blend in with the night?

After a short deliberation, I was pretty certain dark clothes were the order of the day – or night – so I threw on black jeans, dark blue socks, a black tee and a black hoodie with small green dancing bears on the front, then went hunting for my black sneakers. I knew I'd worn them at the park the day we chased the blackmailer but couldn't remember where I'd toed them off when I arrived home. Finally, I found them under the bed gathering dust bunnies and with mud still caked around the heel. Cleaning my sneakers kept me busy for another fifteen minutes.

At precisely 10.30, I switched off all the lights as though going to bed, then lifted the bedroom curtain, just high enough to check on Hudson. As I plastered my nose to the glass, I could see the young Greek guy from the other end of the street walking past with his muscly white and black bull terrier – probably just got home from the deli where he worked with his dad – a white van and two cars cruising past. By the dim glow of the street light I could just make out the *McInerny Schnauzer Kennels* logo on the side of the white van. Mmm…maybe they were visiting the family in the next street who'd bought a show pup from them at the beginning of the year.

I waited until there was no one else in sight. No more pedestrians. No traffic. Not even a stray dog. Just the police car parked in the same spot, nestled up against the curb and by squinting, I could make out a dark shape sitting in the front seat.

"Sorry, Hudson," I whispered as I checked my two lockpicks, Harry and Meghan, were safely tucked inside the back pocket of my jeans along with my phone, then, shielding the torch light with one hand, I felt my way to the back door. Busta, tail wagging in anticipation, trotted along beside me.

"You can't come, sweetie," I told him leaning down to ruffle his ears. "But if you stay really quiet, I'll take you to the dog park in the morning and you can play with your friends. Okay?"

That's if I wasn't locked up in a jail-cell by morning.

With my heart playing leap-frog with my tonsils, I opened the back door, slowly, slowly, so it didn't creak, closed and locked it from the outside and bent to slip the key under the nearest flower pot – just in case I lost the key in my travels and couldn't get back into the house. A scenario that would prove rather difficult to explain to Constable Driscoll.

The six modern units in my block each came with a pocket-sized back yard, a miniscule flower patch, a neat folding clothes line and a galvanized iron fence which divided one unit from the next. As I was neither a mountain goat nor a gym junkie – and sitting at a computer for six hours a day sipping coffee and scoffing chocolate Tim Tam biscuits wasn't exactly a remedy for keeping fit – I dragged a three-step ladder across to the fence to help me navigate fence number one. Okay, if Hudson decided to patrol my backyard while I was away, I'd have some questions to answer, but the only way I could sneak out without being seen was to climb five fences and come out on the next street. Hence, assistance to get started on the first one was a priority.

Did I say *five* fences? Not happening. With no ladder for the next two, by the time I landed with a bump and a smothered curse over fence number three, I was bruised, spitting dirt and something that tasted a lot worse than dirt due to landing in the compost heap and with no strength left to tackle a bump in the ground let alone two more dividing fences.

So, aborting plan A, I staggered to my feet and limped across the yard, hatching plan B on the way. Okay, I'd cross the last two units via their front lawn and pray Hudson wasn't checking out his rear vision mirror at the time.

Unable to switch on my torch in case the couple inside the unit watching some old black and white Humphry Bogart movie spotted the moving light, I slunk past the window, through the side gate and out onto the front lawn. Where I stopped, grabbed a quick breath. Then, before continuing on, I stood for a breathless ten seconds, immobile, while checking the stationary police car and the surroundings for signs of movement.

All good.

Then, just as I turned, ready to traverse the next two lawns, the driver's side door of the police vehicle opened and I froze in mid step. No, no, no. This wasn't happening. Hudson, lithe and controlled as a wild panther, stepped out of the car onto the footpath.

Had he seen me?

I watched him turn his head slowly in my direction. Immediately my breath, or what was left of it, caught in my throat, almost choking me as I struggled to suppress a coughing fit. Luckily, before I could die due to lack of oxygen, he turned his head in the other direction. I watched him stretch his arms up, out to the side, touch his toes ten times and then finish off his exercises by jogging around the car twice, before sliding back into his vehicle and closing the door.

Phew!

Without waiting for the biker-turned-cop to settle in or check his rear-view mirror, I sprinted across the last two front lawns and ducked around the corner into the next street where I bent over double, gasping to catch my breath. Fair dinkum, if I survived tonight's adventure, first thing tomorrow, I was becoming a fully paid-up member of whatever local gym would accept me.

Finally, with one last fortifying breath, I hobbled toward our rendezvous – the solitary red public phone box half-way down the street.

But Dana's dark blue SUV wasn't parked where it was supposed to be and it was already ten minutes past our arranged meeting time. After checking the empty road, both ways, I huddled up against the phone box to wait. A chill which had nothing to do with the cold night air, took root in my chest and left me feeling boneless.

Had the other two *Chicks* called off the mission, deciding it was too dangerous?

18

I held the pay phone to my ear, the cord curled around my finger, and turned my back. If Hudson came barreling around the corner, he might think I was merely a love-struck female who'd misplaced her mobile phone and couldn't get to sleep without a goodnight chat with her boyfriend.

When a couple of minutes passed and no furious cop appeared, I breathed a sigh of relief and returned the phone to the cradle. What now? No way could I get to the Hamilton-Davies' house on my own. My car, locked in the carport, was under the eagle eye of Constable Driscoll and even if it wasn't, I had no intention of breaking in and hunting for clues on my own. Hey, I was a shy romance writer – not Buffy the Vampire Slayer. I blew out a deep sigh at the thought of the fence climbing that lay ahead if I was to return to my unit now, and I swear my sore muscles gave a silent scream of horror.

Still huddled inside the phone box, I peered up the road, calling on the Universe, the God of Cabbage-leaves and any other deity who happened to be listening, to invoke their magic and call up Dana's dark blue SUV with a flick of their wand.

I peered up the road. Nothing. Not even a horse and cart to the rescue. And then, just when I was ready to salute the Universe via my middle finger, two bright headlights cut through the darkness and Dana's SUV slowed down and stopped beside me. I let out a whoop, and the moment Abi leaned across and opened the door, I took a dive out of the phone booth and into the back seat before the mirage could turn into a pumpkin.

"What kept you?" All thumbs, I fumbled to fasten my seat belt while concurrently fist-pumping, doing a sit-down jig, and growling at Dana for her tardiness.

"Jake." *Of course.* "He lost Doggo. I was almost out the door when he woke up screaming for Doggo. Took us fifteen minutes of frantic hunting before Peter eventually discovered the battered and slightly damp stuffed toy in the shower recess and then another fifteen minutes to lull Jake back to sleep."

"Pooh!" Abi, nose scrunched in an oh-my-god-what's-that-smell, leaned away from me as far as her seat belt allowed. "What you been rolling in, Molly?"

"Compost. Detective Lightfoot was as good as his word. There's a police car stationed outside my unit, so I had to climb a few fences to get out undetected." I shook my head. "And you wouldn't want to know some of the stuff people store in their backyards."

Abi, nose still squished, reached across and removed what looked like part of a bush from my hair. "Didn't think Lightfoot would be that quick to react." She wound down the window and let the greenery float out into the night air.

I stifled a grin. "And guess who's sitting in the police car?"

"Chris Hemsworth," said Dana.

I laughed. "You always say that."

"Hey, just because I'm married doesn't mean I'm blind."

"Was it one of the men in blue that responded to the Mayor's death?" asked Abi.

I shook my head. "He's a new constable in town. A guy who was transferred from Salisbury to Port Adelaide station last week." I held my breath, waiting, but there was no way they'd guess the answer to this one. "His name is Constable Hudson Driscoll."

Dana took her eyes off the road long enough to give me an open-mouthed gasp. "Not *your* Hudson Driscoll?"

"Well, I don't know if he's actually *mine*, but yes, Harry's son."

"He's a policeman?"

"And I'm still not sure whether to be mad at him for forgetting to slip this piece of data into the conversation, like the first time he knocked on my door, intent on weaseling information out of me about his father's murder."

"Awkward." Dana guided the SUV around a slow-moving car bearing the number plates SNAIL 00.

"Anyway, he was pretty gung-ho about me locking all my doors and windows and to use flashing lights or ring him at the first sign of trouble."

"Made you feel safe?"

"Yeah, until I had to climb three fences to get away from him."

By now we were turning into Acacia Avenue, two streets along from Jacaranda Avenue. There was a small park on the corner where we left the car, partly hidden by a trough of trees, and hot-footed it to the rear of the Hamilton-Davies' property.

"Oh, my, God, this isn't a fence. This is Trump's Wall." Abi stood peering up at the fence, shaking her head. "It's at least five foot high."

"You can do it." I spoke from experience as I shone my torch on the recess further down, a recess that looked a little easier to navigate than the straight up and down barrier in front of us.

"Quick!" hissed Dana from behind me. "I can see two people turning the corner. We need to be on the other side of that fence before they reach here." And with that she grabbed the top of the fence with both hands, hauled herself up and disappeared from sight. All we heard was a thud and a grunt from the other side.

"Want a leg up?" I said turning to Abi.

"Hey, if Dana can do it, so can I."

"Not necessarily. Unlike us, Dana's an active member of a gym, plus she chases Jake and Kayla every day. What do you chase? Other than Buffy reruns on Netflix?"

"Good point." Abi nodded while I clasped my hands in front of me and when she put her foot in the groove, gave her a lift like I'd seen grooms give jockeys when helping them onto a horse. Abi disappeared over the top followed by a muffled yelp as she landed.

No time to waste. The couple walking down the street were illuminated half way down by a street light, so, flexing my already aching muscles, I latched onto the top of the fence and pulled myself up and over. Not a pretty sight.

But at least we were inside the Hamilton-Davies' property.

Voices could be heard approaching on the other side of the fence.

"I tell you I saw someone standing here a minute ago," said a whiney-sounding female voice from the other side of the fence.

Abi froze, eyes wide, mouth even wider, while Dana placed one finger to her lips and shook her head as I covered my mouth in an attempt to stop a rebel cough from escaping. It tickled my throat and stuck pins in my tonsils as I buried my head inside my bag to minimize any sound.

"No one here!" Voice number two came from an adolescent male with an acute case of inflection-itis.

"I tell you I saw someone."

"Musta been zapped up by space invaders!"

"Should we ring the police?"

"Are you crazy? Come on, babe, let's go. Dicko'll run outta beer iffen we don't hurry!"

As they moved further away and their voices faded, I pulled my head out of the bag and breathed in a lungful of welcome fresh air before trailing Dana and Abi along a narrow path which led to the crime scene, the patio, where the Mayor had taken his last gurgling gasp. I shivered, imagined I could smell blood, as the light from my torch illuminated the body-shaped diagram on the gray pavers.

Dana must have noticed my hesitancy. She crowded up behind me, pushing me toward the double glass doors, the rear entrance to the Hamilton-Davies' rambling home. "Okay, Molly, this is your moment of glory. Time to get to work."

Two minutes later, I narrowed my eyes as I strained to distinguish between the keyhole and the doorframe. "Abi, can you please keep the torch still? I can't find the keyhole."

"I'm cold and you're taking too long."

My knees, digging into the sharp gravel, had gone numb and my shoulders tighter than guitar strings. I let out a quick whoosh, wiggled one shoulder and then the other and decided crime was definitely not a vocation I'd add to my job resume.

To add to the problem, my lock picks seemed to be having an off-day. For the first minute I'd been jiggling Meghan every which way, but as she was being a right royal diva and refusing to cooperate, I'd changed to Harry. Now, with the torchlight flitting everywhere except on the lock, Harry was having a devil of a job even locating the hole.

"Here, give it to me," said Dana swiping the torch from Abi's hand and shining it directly where needed. "Abs, you do a quick reconnaissance, scout around for signs of an open window or unlocked door, you know, in case Molly's lockpicks have gone on strike."

"They're probably as nervous as I am," I mumbled, ticking off in my head the number of crimes we were currently committing. Trespassing. Ignoring the crime-scene tape across the door. Breaking and entering. And acting like we knew what we were doing when we were actually rank amateurs.

I chewed on my bottom lip and kept jiggling. Up-down, down-up, left-right, right-left. It always looked so easy on YouTube videos and I'd had success opening my own front door at home. Might have something to do with the fact that this door belonged to someone else and the little angel on my left shoulder kept yelling at the devil on my right shoulder, reminding him the food in jail was inedible.

"Here we go!" I let out a stifled yell of success as Harry finally clicked into position, I turned the handle and the glass door opened.

"Abi, stop looking, we're in," Dana, whisper-shouted before shouldering the door fully open, leaving me to give Harry a light kiss before stashing him in my back pocket with the now-sulking Meghan, and follow Dana's torchlight into the house.

"Hmm…not bad." Abi trooped through the doorway behind us, eyeballing the large well-equipped games room.

"They certainly enjoy the finer things in life." I shone my torch on the obviously new snooker table and wall-sized television set up as a gaming console with two luxury gaming chairs positioned in front. Obviously, the Mayor and Mayoress, not content with conflict in their daily lives, had enjoyed going against each other in battle games as well. I flashed the torch over the other side of the room where a comfortable lounge suite, a fridge, a bar and a 1970's juke box finished off the setting.

"The office is probably the best place to look," said Abi opening a door that led into the long passageway we'd traversed the day before. "That's if I can remember which door. I was really only trailing along behind Rhianna and my mind was on other things at the time."

I peered into the darkness of the passage and gave my weakening torch a shake. It merely grew weaker. Some detective I was – didn't even check and change my torch batteries before leaving home. "Can't we turn on the passage light? I can't see more than a foot in front of me."

Dana gave a snort. "And get those nosy neighbors next door popping in to check for burglars?"

"Good point. So, what are we looking for?"

Abi's voice floated back from further along the passage. "Something that Michael could have copied or downloaded a photo or video onto." There was a soft thump ahead that sounded like Abi bumping into something solid. "Hey, I think this is the door to the office." She rattled the handle. "Damn, it's locked. Better get your lock picks out again, Molly."

I rolled my eyes – not that anyone could see – and tugged Meghan out from my back pocket. "Okay, let's see what you can do this time," I told her. "Can't let Harry take all the accolades. You've gotta dig in there, girl, show us what you can do. Okay?"

Down on my knees again, I slid Meghan into the keyhole and began the intricate task of following YouTube videos that were playing on a continual loop inside my head. Bingo. Two minutes and the door opened. I grinned down at the productive lock pick. So that was her little secret – she needed to be praised, flaunted, given the royal treatment to secure her cooperation. Whatever. I stood up and returned the instrument to my back pocket where I'm sure I heard her taunting Harry, and led the way into the office.

The computer Rhianna had been using when we'd been sitting in the hard wooden chairs on the other side of her desk was gone. "Looks like the police have already been at work here."

"Yeah, but do they know what to look for?" said Dana. "Do they know Michael was a blackmailer?"

"Maybe there's a USB somewhere around they missed." Abi, tugging open the top drawer of the desk, shone the torch from her phone inside. I could see her sorting through articles inside the drawer before returning them to their original position.

I fished out my phone and clicked it on. Maybe the phone's torch would be stronger than the weak beam coming from my normal torch. Not really knowing what I was looking for, I flashed the light around the room, onto the bookshelves, the filing cabinet in the corner which Dana was attempting to open via a letter-opening knife she'd found God-knows-where, and a small wooden desk on the other side of the room – an antique by the look of it.

I felt my way across the hollow-sounding floorboards and shone the light from my phone on the desk. Beautifully carved. Probably cost more than a couple month's mortgage from whichever leading auction-house they'd unearthed it. I examined it more closely. On top of the desk sat a fine silver fountain pen, a pair of reading glasses, and a *Betty Boop* writing pad. My eyes widened. Was this the clue to Harry's death threat?

At the same moment I reached for the pad, my phone rang in my hand, almost giving me a heart attack. I looked down at the name of my contact. "Oh my God," I whispered, shaking my head at Abi and Dana, "It's Hudson. What'll I do?"

"Pretend you're waking up and you're still half asleep," Abi advised, closing the drawer and coming closer.

Dana, letter-opener half-raised, stopped what she was doing and peered across at me. "Put the phone on speaker so we can all hear."

Hudson was more than likely checking on me to see if everything was okay. I took a deep breath, cleared my throat which had become scratchy and difficult to use as a voice transmitter, before answering. "H-Hi Hudson. Um…hope this is important. You've woken me up and you know I need my beauty sleep."

"Cut the crap, Molly." His voice was steel. "You're not home. I knocked and the noise your dog's making inside the house could wake the dead."

"Umm…"

"So, if you're inside the Hamilton-Davies' house – get out! Pronto! Their neighbors rang the police after seeing lights moving around inside and I happened to pick the call up on my three-way. Squad cars are on their way to Jacaranda Avenue right now, so I'm estimating you have around three minutes to be as far from that area as possible."

Fear, tasting of sour lemons and vinegar, spilled into my mouth and clogged my throat. "B-but how did you–"

"You're not at home, there's been a break-in reported at the Hamilton-Davies' house, and when you add one and one together, Molly, they usually add up to two. Now go!"

It took barely thirty seconds to exit the house and throw ourselves over the back fence – even though I wasted vital time snagging the writing pad from the top of the antique desk. Then, another thirty seconds of flat-out running to reach Dana's SUV.

But we weren't out of the woods yet.

Even if we were lucky enough to evade the police on their way to the crime scene, there was still a very irate constable to confront when Dana dropped me home.

19

Tires screeched as Dana's right foot hit the accelerator and the SUV jumped over the gutter and shot out of the park and onto the bitumen.

"Go!" shouted Abi her head stuck out the window – all the better to check for police cars.

"What do you think I'm doing?" growled Dana, both hands clutching the wheel so tightly we could be in need of a tire-iron to lever each finger off once we were clear of the area.

I clutched the writing pad to my chest like it was the Holy Grail, our only real clue to solving the two murders. But was it worth being arrested? Worth putting my new relationship with Hudson in jeopardy?

Police sirens, blasting through the night air, could be heard getting closer as Dana yanked the wheel hard and we screeched out of Acacia Avenue and onto the Main road.

Three police cars were bearing down on us from a distance.

Oh. My. God. I could feel my heart clattering around in my chest like a loose screw in a rotary fan. I didn't want to be put in handcuffs. I didn't want the ignominy of a strip search at the police station. I wanted to wake up in my own bed in the morning, snuggled up under my fox terrier quilt – not on a hard bench in a cell under a scratchy blanket that smelled like Lysol.

"Quick! Pull into the car park here at McDonald's," ordered Abi. "If we stay on the road, we might get pulled over."

"Good idea," I gasped, grabbing onto the dashboard with one hand as the car swerved into the food chain's entrance and bumped its way around the back to the parking area. "We can order food, eat inside the café, hide in plain sight."

"And we can unwind," said Dana almost taking out a Toyota's side mirror as she skidded the SUV in between it and a four-wheel drive. "'Cos, I'm as strung out as piano wire."

And it took a lot to 'string out' our designated leader.

"Well, I'm all for ordering a Big Mac, fries, and a strawberry thick shake," said Abi, undoing her seat belt and climbing out of the car. "Fear always makes me extra hungry."

I wasn't sure I could force food down my throat but if we were about to hide in plain sight, we needed to order up big and appear as though we were three normal friends enjoying a late-night supper after a movie – not three crims on the lam, dressed from head to toe in black and bearing stolen property. With the deafening wail of police sirens blasting our ears as they passed by, I steadied the writing pad under my black hoodie and followed the other two *Chicks* through the Golden Arches and into the fast-food cafeteria.

Five minutes later, arms overflowing with shallow but tasty calories, I collapsed on a green plastic chair and arranged our goodies on the table in front of me. I'd collected the three burgers, plus fries, Abi was struggling to carry three thick shakes without dropping the lot and Dana was strolling out of the Ladies loo, her red hair a little less messy than when she went in.

I pushed Dana's burger, Chicken Supreme, and Abi's Big Mac across the table and collapsed on the chair between them, still hanging onto my own chicken burger. "Well, we're safe in here for now, but Hudson will probably be restless so we can't stay long."

As if he'd heard, my phone pinged and a text from Hudson popped up on my screen.

Where are you?

I looked at Abi, then Dana, and held up my phone so they could read the text. "What do I say?" I shrugged one shoulder. "Can't very well say we felt a bit peckish so decided to drop into McDonald's for a feed and did he want fries with his burger."

"Ignore him," advised Abi. "If you tell him the truth – he'll be mad. If you say you're on the way home and you're not there within the next ten minutes – he'll be mad. You can't win either way. So…best not to answer."

Good reasoning. I buried my phone in my back pocket and sunk my teeth into a crispy hot chip. Something about McDonald's chips the world over that beat those made in the oven at home.

"Well," said Abi, licking chocolate shake off her lips with an active tongue and shaking her head. "Sad to say, our mission was a bit of a flop."

"Not completely." I could barely hide my grin.

"But all that danger, and we didn't find a damn thing."

"I did."

Dana's head came up. "You did?"

"I found this!" I unzipped my hoodie, dragged out the writing pad and placed it in the middle of the scattered burger wrappers and almost-empty milk shake containers. And there she was, all curvy and sassy as she beamed up at me from her playful pose at the top of the first page.

Betty Boop.

When I'd snatched the writing pad, I'd thought myself akin to the illustrious Jessica Fletcher, even though my less than professional exit over the Hamilton-Davies' back fence saw me close to face-planting on the footpath on other side. Definitely not a typical Jessica Fletcher move.

Me…Molly Gibson, the least likely sleuth of our *Gumshoe Chicks* investigative team.

But hey, I'd identified and appropriated a valuable clue.

Both Dana and Abi gaped at me. Then Dana's grin matched mine. "You found that in the Hamilton-Davies' house?"

I nodded.

"Our one and only clue?"

I nodded again, starting to feel like one of those bobble-headed dogs you see in the rear of some cars. "Yep. Snagged it off the antique desk in Rhianna's office. Noticed it just before Hudson's phone call but didn't have time to mention it because after that we took off like the boogey man was after us."

Abi picked the writing pad up reverently, like it might disintegrate with handling. "Harry's death threat was torn off a *Betty Boop* writing pad, so, all we have to do is rub the page lightly with a lead pencil and if either Rhianna or Michael wrote that note, it will show up." She grinned at me around a fat, well-cooked fry. "Good for you. And here's me believing romance writers had their heads perpetually buried in the clouds."

"And their hearts in the middle of a love triangle," added Dana, punching me lightly on the arm. I frowned at Dana and she laughed when I returned her punch. "Come on, Molly," she said. "How many romance writers carry lock picks in their back pocket? Let's face it, you, my friend, are not a cookie-cutter cliché." She dug into her mammoth Mummy bag. "Now, I'm sure I have a pencil in here somewhere. I remember Kayla using a pencil to draw alien kittens on the back of a *Fasta Pasta* menu just last week." She pulled out two packets of pineapple juice, a Barbie doll with no head and a packet of hand-wipes before diving in again and removing a stubby lead pencil. "Can't wait to test out your theory."

I had a sudden chilling thought. "But what if you find the incriminating words, 'Harry You're Dead', indented into the paper and it's in Michael's handwriting?" My voice cracked. "Does that mean there's more than one murderer?"

"Maybe we don't want to find out. Maybe we should drop the writing pad in the bin." Abi's shaky voice mirrored my thoughts.

But Dana took the decision away from us. Lead pencil in hand, she attacked the writing pad with gusto and light penciling, making sure to cover every inch of the paper.

And came up with zilch.

She shook her head and sighed. "Not them. It's a new pad."

"So, neither Michael nor Rhianna wrote that death threat," said Abi, disappointment in her voice.

"Unless they used the last page of their old writing pad and then bought this new one." My heart wasn't in it but I guessed that could have happened.

Abi stopped sucking at the last few dregs of her chocolate shake. "So, now we're left with no clues to follow."

She was right. Things were looking bad. We'd hit rock bottom in our investigation.

I stood up, started collecting the empty wrappers to drop in the bin. "Time to leave," I said. "The police should be occupied at the Hamilton-Davies' house by now so it might be a good time to hit the road."

*****

At precisely nine o'clock the following morning, after partaking of coffee and two slices of marmalade-covered toast that I brought out to his car with a contrite smile, Hudson gave a final toot of his horn and disappeared up the street.

Before he left, there'd been no mention of picking me up on his Harley nor showing me his dragon tattoo. No goodbye kiss. No cheeky wink.

Things were still a little strained between us.

When Dana pulled up in front of my unit the night before, Constable Driscoll had little to say, other than informing us how many brands of idiots we were and how close we'd come to being fitted-out for prison uniforms. He didn't mention the fact that if his superiors found out he'd rung to warn us, he could be wearing prison garb himself, but the words, although unsaid, were floating around the air like invisible darts.

I watched Hudson drive up the street and once the police car turned the corner out of sight, I wandered inside, heart heavy. Was our promising relationship already doomed? I'd apologized for being reckless, for putting him on the spot, not a lot else I could do. Guess the ball was now in Hudson's court.

I closed the front door and locked it behind me – couldn't be too careful – and contemplated the day ahead. Writing would take up my morning and I had an author's book-signing event at Dymock's bookshop in the city to attend this afternoon.

Determined to lose myself in my current manuscript, I switched on the computer, made another cup of coffee and settled into the ergonomically designed computer chair that cost more than a trip to Bali, all ready to sort out my fictional characters' love lives – so much easier than in real life.

Tabitha had finally realized Ethan, the fiancé who'd left her at the altar, wasn't worth the mental anguish she'd been putting herself through. Any man who could blithely shrug and walk away from a two-year relationship on the day of his wedding – because he'd rather be single – wasn't worth one more sleepless night. But what about Gray? Was Ethan's bed-hopping best friend ready to change his shallow lifestyle and settle for one woman?

'Gray's eyes flicked to the slinky dame in the silver catsuit and fuck-me red high-heels that he swore were a foot high. She was leaning provocatively against the bar, her eyes, painted in blue black and silver to make them appear larger, sexier, were conveying her willingness to go upstairs and indulge in some naked naughtiness. No strings attached. A pastime his commitment-phobic self normally thrived on. Yet something inside of him closed down. Felt repulsed by this woman, her face harder than a newly fired cement brick, and the blatant sexual messages she conveyed. Strangely, the thought of casual sex with a stranger made his stomach turn. Why? What was happening to him? He took a swig of his drink and looked away. In his mind, another face, devoid of make-up, sweet, lips full and kissable appeared dressed in a shabby bathrobe, her hair in a wrap-around towel. Tabitha. The woman

his best friend tossed aside like a piece of used chewing-gum. The woman he was falling in love with.

He jolted. Almost spilled his drink on the bar counter. Falling in love? Where had that erroneous idea come from? Ever since his mother walked out when he was five and his father, pickled with drink, left him in the care of Welfare on his sixth birthday, Gray had refused to trust his heart to anyone. Easier to boast about the notches in his bedpost and be gone from the rumpled bed before morning. He'd learned early in life love was an emotion that only brought grief and loss. That there must be something wrong with him for the two people who should have loved him the most to pull the plug and walk away.

He was no good for Tabitha. She'd been hurt enough. Best if he ended their relationship now.

Only one way...

Upending his glass and letting the remaining whisky warm his dry throat as it trickled down, he sought out the woman in the slinky catsuit. She was still emitting sexual vibes, eager for free drinks and an hour or two of entertainment. Gray flicked his head, sent her one of those devastatingly cocky grins he'd mastered so well and watched as she licked her lips with the tip of her tongue. He'd made a score.

But why did this feel like he was cutting out his own heart and feeding it to the wolves?

Tamping down his tangled thoughts, he strode towards a night of no-ties-pleasure but at the last moment sidestepped temptation and continued walking out the door and into the night.'

The timer on my desk shrilled, bringing my writing sprint to a close. I quickly re-read the words I'd written, made a couple of changes, pushed my chair back and stood up.

If only Hudson could see the light like her fictional hero, Gray, was beginning to...

"Okay, guys, time to hit the backyard and stretch our legs," I told Flerken and Busta who were both asleep.

Busta, on a feather-filled dog bed no more than three feet from my chair woke up, noticed I'd finished writing and scrambled to his feet, big smile on his face. Flerken, however, from his curled-up position beside my computer, cracked one eye half-open and scowled at me. With a grunt of displeasure, he scrunched himself into a tighter ball and, still scowling, went back to sleep.

During my exhausting fence climbing stint the night before, I'd realized that sitting at the computer writing romance novels was not the best way to keep my body fit. I needed to exercise more. So, instead of paying out an exorbitant amount to join a gym and never go, I'd devised the idea of writing in 30-minute sprints, each sprint followed by some form of exercise. Earlier, I'd run up and down the stairs without stopping, for two minutes – which necessitated my complete and utter collapse on the sofa until I could actually breathe again. This time, I intended exercising out in my miniscule back yard.

While Busta darted around in circles tossing his mutilated yellow tennis ball in the air and catching it again, I decided on thirty push-ups. Looked easy enough on the exercise videos advertised on TV. Down on my knees, I stretched out face first on the ground, spat out a mouthful of damp earth that tasted of fertilizer, positioned my hands in front of me, and began counting.

One…and two…and three…and four…and five…and six…and…

Ugh. I flopped nose first in the dirt, arms, weaker than two celery sticks, refusing to push my body off the ground again.

The videos lied.

Huffing like a worn-out carpet sweeper, I staggered back into the kitchen, just as a car crunched to a halt out the front of my unit. I froze. Had the murderer come to finish me off? Take more threatening photos of me and my vulnerable pets?

A child's shrill squeal, followed by the woof of an excited dachshund, announced the arrival of the *Chicks* and their entourage. An emotion even stronger than pleasure skittered through me as I suddenly realized how much I craved the strength and love of my two best friends, Dana and Abi.

'The Love Triangle' with Tabitha and Gray could wait.

Calling out a greeting, I hurried to unlock the front door, eager to let the gang in. We had lots to talk about. Especially as the *Betty Boop* writing pad I'd pilfered from the antique desk in Rhianne's office had proved a squib. Neither of the Hamilton-Davies' were guilty of ripping a piece off that pad to print out a death threat, plus we'd also failed to find proof of Michael blackmailing the murderer.

Which meant we were now clueless as to what to do next.

"Hey, Moll. Good to see you still in one piece." Abi, a cardboard cake box under one arm and a bright-eyed squirming dachshund tucked under the other, edged through the doorway. "Thought Hudson might have chewed you up into bite-sized chunks after we dropped you off last night."

I touched a hand to my heart. "Are the bite marks still showing?"

She grinned. "Don't worry, he'll come 'round. The guy's besotted with you. Once he calms down, you'll be camped on the back of his Harley, roaring off into the sunset."

Dana surged through the doorway herding a shiny black greyhound and two children in front of her. Kayla, looking sweet in a sparkly fairy costume and Jake, clutching Doggo to his chest while shouting something completely unintelligible to everyone except himself and bouncing up and down like a constipated kangaroo.

From the corner of my eye, I spotted Flerken. My cat was now wide awake and hissing his annoyance. One pained glare in Jake's direction and he was off the desk, across the room and on top of the refrigerator, his fallback plan whenever the exuberant toddler arrived at our house. With another glare at the bouncing kangaroo who'd taken over my living room, the ginger cat let out a give-me-strength sigh, before curling up beside a half-used tissue box to monitor proceedings from on high.

"Coffee?" I said, automatically turning the kettle on before trundling across the room to save and close down my current document before turning the computer off. No more writing for me this morning, but I wasn't fussed. Dana and Abi were much better company at the moment than a weirded out Gray and an over-emotional Tabitha.

"Hey, lookee here – I've brought donuts!" Abi dropped the cardboard box on the table before carefully placing Chloe on the floor. The dachshund, ears flapping, immediately bounced across to Busta's toy box, snatched Pooh, his favorite toy, and eyes glinting with mischief, dived under the sofa. Busta, whose shrill barks of excitement were making my eyes water, went skidding across the room ready to play, while Penelope looked on with interest, waiting to see if Pooh bear squeaked before deigning to join their game.

I let out a laugh and shook my head. A typical chaotic *Chicks* entrance.

"These looked yummy," I said, lifting the lid off Abi's cardboard box and peering in at the dozen ultra-fresh donuts, all iced in different colors.

Abi snaffled a chocolate covered treat. "Thought we could do with the extra sugar. I'm still shaking from last night's near-miss."

I shuddered. "If it hadn't been for Hudson's warning…"

Neither of us needed to finish my sentence. I shivered again at the thought of how close we'd come to getting caught red-handed breaking into the Hamilton-Davies' house. And all for nothing.

Dana, who was busy slipping a DVD into the player at the other end of my open plan lounge-kitchen, called out, "Did Hudson have anything else to say after we left?"

"You mean did he elaborate on calling us idiots and how close we'd come to being fitted-out for prison uniforms?'

"Yeah, that." The moment *Cats and Dogs 2* appeared on the TV screen, Dana dumped a squirming Jake in the middle of a squashy beanbag, righted Kayla's tipping tiara and dug into her family-sized bag for two small juice packets which she distributed to her offspring before joining us. "Thought he'd self-combust when we first pulled up," she said snaffling a donut from the box. "And you must admit he has a way with words. I didn't know there were so many different adjectives to describe 'idiots'."

Ab raised one eyebrow. "Thought *scaremongering* idiots was a good one."

"Yeah, and how about *zombie-brained*? Pretty original, wouldn't you say?"

I set three large coffee mugs on the table next to the donuts and let out a sigh. Didn't know which was worse – Hudson yelling last night or giving me the silent treatment this morning. Although he did thank me for the coffee and toast and come to think of it, he tooted his horn before leaving. "Thank God you insisted we wear gloves, Dana. Just think, if we'd left fingerprints at the scene of the crime, Hudson could have been outed for ringing to warn us."

"And *we'd* be sitting in a jail cell using a bucket for a toilet," added Abi, pausing from licking chocolate off her fingers to digest that horrifying thought.

"So," said Dana, one eye on Jake who was riding his beanbag like a rodeo bull while giggling at the antics of the dogs acting on television. "What did we learn from last night's mission?"

Abi shrugged one shoulder. "That breaking into houses is a definite no-no?"

"That we need to develop a better fence-hopping technique?" I carried the bruises to promote that one.

Dana shook her head. "And what about the gloves? Doesn't that prove that the *Gumshoe Chicks* are becoming more professional in their investigations?"

But what about the fact that we'd put ourselves in more danger by actually breaking into the Hamilton-Davies' house in the first place? Gloves or no gloves? I frowned at Dana who'd helped herself to a strawberry donut and was waving it in the air like a conductor at a music festival. "So," I said, drawing the word out. "You don't think we're idiots for going off half-cocked? And that breaking into houses is for criminals and not investigators?"

Dana stopped waving her donuts and as though pricked of all air, dropped heavily into a kitchen chair, shoulders sagging.

"No…well…maybe. But it seemed like a good idea at the time."

"Yeah…"

I pushed a mug of coffee – milk and two sugars – across the table and collapsed on the chair beside her. "Still we *did* find one clue."

Abi breathed out a deep meaningful sigh. "Even if it was a fizzer."

"Look at it this way," said Dana, shifting into a straighter posture and producing a perky face. "Clues that don't work out can still be of great value to an investigation. To me, this means we can eliminate both Rhianna and Michael from our enquiries."

"But aren't you forgetting something?" I pushed the words through cold lips. "Michael Hamilton-Davies had already been eliminated. He's dead. Bumped off by whoever killed Harry, probably for getting greedy and cocky and resorting to blackmail."

Abi shook her head. "And even though we broke into the house last night we're still no closer to the identity of the killer."

A bone-deep coldness, enhanced with razor-sharp icicles impaled my intestines. I shivered. "Yeah…and that same killer is still threatening us."

"Which means, we need to find out who he or she is." Dana dug into her mammoth bag and pulled out a small yellow grocery-pad and a biro. "Before they kill again." She settled more comfortably in her chair and poised the biro over the pad. "So…what do we have?"

"No clues," said Abi with a dismal shrug.

"No evidence," I added, dolefully curling a piece of hair around one finger.

"Okay, so we failed in our mission last night." Dana gave us both one of her growly-faced Mum-looks that she used to control her two offspring. "Get over it. We have to move on. Now, who haven't we checked off our list yet? And what's our next plan?"

"The McInerneys," said Abi.

I nodded. "And we need a damn good excuse to go see them."

The icy coldness attacked me again as the unsaid words continued on in my brain…*because otherwise they might pay us a visit first.*

20

Dymocks bookshop in Adelaide was holding a book-signing for *'Kama Sutra Surprise'*, the latest of my romance novels to be published and I wanted to look 'authorly' – if there is such a word. Last time I did an event with two other authors, one a YA writer and the other a Paranormal, I'd come off looking less like a romance writer and more like Mrs. Potts Goes to Town.

I'd worn a beige pants suit with a muted orange shirt and, thinking it would make me look more like a writer, donned a pair of glasses – clear glass – that I'd found on eBay, while the YA writer, a woman in her late fifties had dressed like one of her teenager readers in a flamboyant outfit of short denim booty shorts and a boob tube with one of those cute little gold rings hanging off her belly button. Even more ostentatious, the Paranormal author could have been mistaken for a participant in a Halloween parade.

This time, I worked on my make-up and after three changes of clothes finally decided on an outfit I'd bought for an end-of-year party I'd chickened out on at the last minute because I didn't want to be seen attending without a partner. It consisted of a pretty white dress with miniscule pink flowers and a dreamy swirly skirt that finished an inch above my knees. To finish off, I tied a soft pink scarf loosely around my neck then dug into my shoe box and came out with a cute pair of white wedged sandals.

As I closed the door behind me and walked to my little red car, I actually felt like a bona fide romance writer. I was looking forward to signing books and chatting to my readers. In fact, the plot for my most popular romance book, *Sweet Hydrangea,* had been suggested by one of my readers at a book-signing, two years ago.

The smell of good coffee greeted me as I swished through Dymock's front door and set myself up at a small table in the romance section of the bookshop. Couldn't wait to take the first sip of that coffee. Some good fairy must have sourced it from a nearby Starbucks.

"Hi, I'm Jodi Chamberlain – your assistant for today. Anything you need, Ms. Gibson, you only have to ask." The good fairy, (bookseller), a tiny vivacious pixie of a woman in her mid-forties, sent me a genuine smile as I settled at the table behind a pile of my books plus several biros and a fountain pen.

"Please, call me Molly."

Her smile widened. "I love your books, Miss…um…Molly. Sometimes I stay up reading until the early hours of the morning. Of course, then I'm late for work and get into trouble." She sighed. "But reading about your hunky bad boy heroes and the beautiful but strong heroines who tame them and show that love is the key to happiness, makes it all worthwhile."

Geez, I could use this woman to market my books. Instead, I smiled, lifted a copy of *Kama Sutra Surprise* from the stack on the table, opened to the title page and signed, 'To Jodi Chamberlain, my favorite fan', before passing the book across to her.

Already, a line of people were snaking down the romance aisle of the bookstore, so after a few sips of coffee, I settled into the comfortable cushion adorned chair, selected a watermelon pink biro with silver sparkles from the stash, and beamed at the lady heading the line-up, a sweet-faced octogenarian complete with white hair, stooped shoulders, and a walking frame. A copy of *Kama Sutra Surprise* clasped tightly between her arthritic fingers, she shuffled forward to the table and dropped the book in front of me.

"Sebastian, that bad boy of yours, woohoo, he can put his boots under my bed any night of the year." Her sassy grin said her outside appearance might be wrinkled and worn, but her inner passion was still alive and kicking.

Two hours later, with the line down to a trickle, I broke off to stand, stretch and contemplate a visit the Ladies' Rest Room. That second cup of coffee, fully drained an hour ago, was definitely asking to be set free.

"Won't be long," I told the half-dozen readers still waiting in line for their book to be signed. "Chat to each other while I'm gone. Author signings are a great way to make friends with like-minded readers."

By the time I followed Jodi's convoluted directions and found the Rest Room, I was almost at the stage of walking cross-legged. Thankfully, there was an empty cubicle waiting for me.

As I finished up, I heard the Rest room door open and then voices outside my cubicle. "It is," said one high-pitched voice.

"Isn't," said a second even-squeakier voice.

"It's that woman we saw at the *Pampered Pooch*. The one with the uncontrollable mutt."

"Doesn't look like her at all."

"Oh, Bitzy, you need new glasses. I told you two weeks ago to get your eyes tested."

"Nothing wrong with my eyes, Trixie. The woman with the scary little dog we saw at *Pampered Pooch* was at least six foot tall. This one's only a shrimp."

"Is not."

"Is so."

Oh, my, God. Was that the Bobbsey Twins? The two sisters from Abi's boutique with the ancient smelly dogs? What in heck were they doing at Dymock's bookshop? Surely, they weren't romance readers.

Unable to put it off any longer, I flushed, straightened my dress, and pushed open the cubicle door.

And there they were. So alike, even if they told me, I'd never remember which was which.

"Told you so," said Twin One, then, with a lift of her sharp pointy nose she turned to me. "You're a *Gumshoe Chick*, aren't you? Just like our friend, Abi Truelove?"

I smiled and nodded as I turned on the tap to wash my hands.

"And you're investigating that poor man's death at the dog show," said Twin Two – might have been Trixie.

I nodded again, pressed the button on the dryer before letting the warm air blow over my hands. "Were you two ladies at the show the day of Harry's murder?"

"Of course," said might-have-been Trixie. "We may not compete any more but we still meet up with friends at the show quite regularly."

"Don't suppose you saw anything out of the ordinary that day? Anything that might help with our investigation?" I asked, expecting a negative shake of the head but hey, if the ladies were at the show, it was worth a try. "We're a bit short of clues at the moment."

"Now, let me see…who was it we saw with blood on his shirt?" mused Twin One.

Blood? My ears instantly pricked and began to waggle, while she screwed up her already wizened face and tipped her head to the side.

She scratched at the hair under her nose. "Was it the ice-cream vendor?"

"No, no, it was the hot dog man."

"Was not."

"Was so."

I blinked. They'd seen someone with blood on their shirt and they hadn't thought to mention this before?

Twin One tugged her tatty fawn cardigan more closely around her bony body. "I do remember one thing though, he was young."

"Well, it can't be the hot dog man," said Twin Two with a shake of her head. "He's older than Methuselah. Not a tooth left in his head and his hands are clawed with arthritis. How he manages to squeeze the sauce bottle on his hot dogs, I can't imagine." Twin Two lifted one finger. "But I do recall, when we stopped the young man, I advocated using *Cleanout* to remove the blood stains."

"No, no, it wasn't you – it was me. I told him to use *Bloodaway*. Remember, I saw the commercial on television the week before where the woman's dress had a stain right down the front from a nose bleed and after one squirt of *Bloodaway* and a twenty-minute soak in cold water she could have worn that dress to a Governor's dinner."

"The young lad with the blood-stained shirt said he'd had a nose bleed too."

I jumped in before Twin Two distracted her sister with more contradictions re the hot dog man's arthritis. "Can you remember his name?"

"Hmm…let me see…was it, Gregory?"

"No, it was Steven."

Twin Two rubbed a gnarly finger along the side of her nose. "Or was it, Jeffery?"

"Ah…I remember, it was Jason."

Twin Two clapped her hands together and laughed so hard she dislodged her false teeth. "Yes, yes, it was Jason," she said, pushing her uppers back into place. "Jason McInerny. He was running to his car with the blood-stained shirt over his arm – almost took us out in his rush – and he grew quite cross when we stopped to advise him of the correct way to eliminate the blood stains."

"No thanks at all."

"That's because young ones these days are too self-absorbed to listen to advice."

"Not self-absorbed, dear – they're too *social* – you know, with those smart phones."

"Self-absorbed."

"Social."

Well, well, well. I eyed the still-arguing women as I edged my way out of the Ladies Rest Room to return to the book signing. Thanks to the Bobbsey Twins, a very important clue had landed smack bang in my lap.

Jason McInerny, the loser son of the McInerny family who owned the imported giant schnauzer that kept getting beaten by Harry's dog, Scout, had left the show grounds carrying a blood-stained shirt. He'd left before the police arrived and therefore hadn't been questioned.

Why was Jason in such a hurry?

Did he really have a nose bleed?

Or would the blood on his shirt match the blood on the grooming scissors speared deep inside Harry Driscoll's heart?

21

After signing *Kama Sutra Surprise* for the last fan and presenting Jodi with a box of chocolates for her assistance, I decided to drive from the city out to Lewiston to visit *McInerny Kennels*, home to the expensive imported Giant Schnauzer, *UK. Ch. Grumbles of Midsomer* – and the McInerny family.

No way was I going to confront Jason – and be labelled one of those too-stupid-to-live female protagonists who in some books walk blindly into trouble by tackling the murder suspect on her own – but I figured while Jason was at work, this would be a good opportunity to have a little chat with his parents. Ascertain if he really did have a nose bleed the day Harry Driscoll was murdered.

Whenever I visit doggy friends in Lewiston, where many have set up and established their show kennels, I always stop off at the Two Wells bakery. Can't resist it. There's something about country bakeries that prove impossible to drive past. An invisible sign hanging out the front saying, 'Stop here for a taste of Heaven'.

Two Wells was a semi-country town that was fast becoming more populated as the suburbs spread further outwards from the city of Adelaide. As I parked in front of the shop, the scent of newly baked bread flooded the car, the yeasty aroma drifting in through the open windows. After texting both Dana and Abi to fill them in on my latest clue – Jason McInerny's blood-stained shirt – I drew in one long intoxicating lungful of cinnamon and chocolate cookies, fresh from the oven, and waited for an answer. A strategy we'd learned from our last investigation when Abi almost died because she didn't keep the other two *Chicks* fully informed and ended up facing the killer alone.

I sat in the car, salivating, the heady smells of apple pie and gingerbread wafting through the window, until both Dana and Abi returned my message: Dana with a 'thumbs-up' emoticon and Abi with a text, 'Good work, Nancy Drew. Meeting at my place 7.00pm tonight.'

Hopefully, by then, I'd have more findings to report after grilling Jason's parents.

A Cornish pasty for my dinner was the reason I'd stopped at the bakery, but after sitting in the car being bombarded by drool-inducing smells, I ended up with not only a pasty but a custard tart, six chocolate cookies and a cinnamon roll that jumped up and waved at me when I strolled through the door.

In the middle of activating my card on the Tap-and-Go machine and collecting my bags full of *yum*, my phone rang.

Hudson.

What now? More shellacking? More disappointment? Phone pressed to my ear and three white paper bags clutched in the other hand, I pushed the bakery door open with my shoulder. There was something about Hudson that made me want to cut through the silence and re-find the warmth. After all, I did put him in a precarious position last night by sneaking away when he was in charge of guarding me. "Hi Hudson. What's up?"

"Just ringing to say I'm sorry for yelling at you and I really like you, Molly." He was gabbling, as though he wanted to get his words in quickly before I could interrupt. "But there's a killer out there – he's already murdered my dad – and when I found out you were in danger, where I couldn't protect you…I-I lost it. And, I'm sorry."

I stopped suddenly, causing the woman behind me, weighed down with an armful of bakery bags, to slam into my back and drop one of her bags resulting in several pastry puffs, overflowing with cream, to hit the pavement and smash.

"Oh, Hudson, that's okay and I'm so glad you rang." I bent down to help the lady who was waving her arms, shouting, her apoplectic face red with horror at the sight of her ruined cream puffs. Damn. I couldn't very well continue talking on the phone and leave her to sort out the mess. She'd have a coronary. "Look, I'm in the middle of a minor crisis at the moment, Hudson. It involves squashed cream cakes. Can I get back to you?"

"Where are you?"

"Outside the Two Wells bakery and there's been a slight pastry accident that I need to attend to."

"Can I see you tonight?"

"Will there be a Harley in the mix?"

"If that's what it takes." Fair dinkum, he was almost purring.

"It does. And Hudson…I really like you too," I purred back. "The *Chicks* are meeting at seven, so how about you pick me up afterwards, around nine-ish?"

By now the red-faced lady looked ready to swing a punch, so I quickly said my goodbyes and hastened to assure her we'd go back into the shop, buy more cream puffs to replace those presently dying on the pavement, and I'd foot the bill. But first I had to ensure my own bakery stash remained undamaged by stowing them on the passenger seat of my car. Cream Puff lady, determined I wasn't going to renege on the deal and jump in my car and drive off, tagged me all the way.

Ten minutes later, after replacing the woman's goodies and cleaning up the mess on the pavement, helped by the long agile tongue of an obliging dog – a mixture of corgi, bull terrier and something that could have been a dachshund with abnormally long legs – I was back in the car and heading away from Two Wells toward Lewiston and the *McInerny's Schnauzer Kennels.*

As I drove, I sang along with the radio. Not normal for a person in the middle of a murder investigation and with a killer intent on upping his killer count, but hey, Hudson had rung, apologized and was picking me up tonight on his Harley. *And* he really liked me. Something that had been missing in the few short dysfunctional relationships I'd been in so far. Something I thought would never happen to me. By the time I pulled up outside *McInerny's Schnauzer Kennels* I'd sung along with all the songs I knew on 5AD radio and if I didn't know the words, I made them up.

Funny what love – or even *maybe*-love – can do to the way you feel inside.

I drove the car into the driveway past a carved bush in the shape of a Schnauzer and parked between a 10-dog trailer with the *McInerny Kennels* logo on both sides and their white work van with the same logo. The same van I'd seen driving past my unit the night before when I was checking on Hudson through the window. I looked around. The only clues these people were in financial trouble, due to their expensive imported stud dog being ignored by breeders, was the shabby curtains at the windows, the lack of thread on a couple of the trailer tires and the fact the Schnauzer bush was badly in need of a trim. The dog's bushy beard was longer than Rip Van Winkle's.

I rapped on the front door, two fingers on my other hand tightly crossed in case Jason had decided to have a day off work due to a sore shoulder caused by whacking poor Michael Hamilton-Davies over the head with a shovel.

A rusty high-pitched yapping from behind the door greeted my knock. Definitely not the deep throaty bark of a Giant Schnauzer. I waited, heart performing a Hulu dance inside my chest. Hitting Jason's parents with questions re their killer son seemed like a good idea from the comfort and safety of my car. Now, not so much.

The door opened and Mr. McInerny, dressed in a crumpled shirt, dirty jeans and socks with two of his toes poking through holes stood staring down at me from his 6-foot-plus height while a grizzled geriatric chihuahua, who, although on tottery legs, still thought he was a Rottweiler, stood guard at the man's feet. Mr. McInerny frowned and then something between recognition and surprise passed behind his eyes and his mouth turned up into a smile. "I know you, don't I? Seen you around the dog shows. Come in! Come in!" He stepped aside and ushered me into the house with one hand.

"I'm Molly Gibson," I said following him and his dog down a passage lined with cardboard boxes overflowing with shredded paper and into a large kitchen area at the rear of the house. "Just wondered if you had time to answer a few questions about Jason."

His smile widened as he pulled out a kitchen chair and indicated I sit at the table. "Has that son of mine been playing tag with your heart?" He shook his head, all sympathy. "Young ones today. Think it's a game to flit from one relationship to the next without a moment's pause."

"Um…no…" Oh God, I couldn't very well tell the poor guy there was no way I'd ever be interested in Jason as a lover but I suspected his son of murder and was here to ask for his help to prove it. "Umm…but I did sort of have a couple of questions…"

"Say no more. I'll speak to Jason tonight. Now, do you take milk and sugar? I was just about to have my afternoon tea." He looked vaguely around the kitchen as though expecting someone to appear like a genie from a bottle and make the hot drinks for us. However, the only other living creature was the geriatric dog, who'd collapsed as though exhausted, onto his bed of blankets in front of the stove. "Um…hang on, I think there might be some jellied donuts in the cupboard." He switched the kettle on before fumbling around inside a walk-in pantry, presumably hunting for donuts.

"Someone told me Jason had a nose bleed at the dog show last weekend," I said, trying to make my voice sound conversational rather than accusatory. "Does he suffer from them often?"

Mr. McInerny's head popped out of the cupboard, a frown ridged deeply between his eyes.

"It's just that I…um…I used to suffer from nose bleeds myself as a child," I blustered, my mouth taking over from my brain. "At the time, my doctor recommended cauterization, you know, a hot needle up the nose to seal the blood vessels and build scar tissue – and-and it worked."

I gulped down a dry lump in my throat. "Um…maybe that might help Jason."

"I'll pass the information on to him." The frown was still there as he selected two mugs from a mug-tree in the middle of the kitchen table. He held up a chipped *Tweety-bird* mug. "This one do?"

"Love it," I said, forcing a smile on my face while trying to work out how I could continue asking questions about Jason's killer instincts without his father pouring hot tea over me for accusing his son of murder. "I see you collect pretty mugs."

Mr. McInerny's face softened. "Not me, but my wife does…did."

Oh God, did Mrs. McInerny die? And here was me accusing his son of murder. I was a monster. An uncaring monster who didn't deserve his offer of tea and cake.

"She's not here now," he went on, his eyes looking around the room as though suddenly surprised by her absence. "Left me one month two days and three hours ago."

Left him as in *died*? Or left him as in *took off*? I squirmed on the chair. Possibly time to change the subject. "How did your dogs go at the show last weekend? Any ribbons?"

He came back to earth with a couple of eye blinks and a sniff, before dropping tea bags into *Tweety-bird* and *Popeye* and filling the mugs with hot water. "Yes, yes, Matilda, one of our minis amassed enough points to claim Champion."

We continued chatting about the dogs while I sipped my tea and eyed the two jellied donuts decorating a less-than-clean plate in the center of the table, with suspicion. How long did he say his wife had been gone? A month? Is that how old these insipid, rubbery-looking creations had been stagnating in the cupboard? Topped with a reddish hard dried concoction that maybe was 'jelly' in another lifetime, but now had the capacity to take out at least one of my teeth if I adhered to my Great Gran's Etiquette rule and forced them down my throat, I passed on the donuts and pondered on how to bring the subject back to his killer son.

The ancient chihuahua huddled in front of the stove lifted its back leg and began a thorough job of cleaning its privates. Every second lick accompanied with a satisfied sort of snort.

"Who do you think murdered Harry Driscoll?" I asked, almost mesmerized by the ritual slurping.

When there was no immediate answer, I looked up. Mr. McInerny was studying the desiccated donut in his hand as though it was as fresh as the day his wife brought it home from the bakery. "Haven't given it much thought," he said and took a huge mouthful which put a stop to any conversation for the next few minutes.

The kitchen appeared to be the hub of the house, as though once his wife left, he couldn't be bothered using any other room. There was even a make-shift folding bed, unmade, parked next to a desk overflowing with papers, dirty cups and unopened envelopes that looked like bills.

I squinted, peered at the writing pad poking out from under a *Fred Flintstone* coffee mug. Was that one of *Betty Boop's* red high-heels I could see? A sexy leg with a red garter? My heart did a little dance as I leaned closer. Checked out the love heart on Betty's garter.

"You make great tea, Mr. McInerny. Any chance of a second cup?" I held up my empty mug and smiled at him. He might be a nice old man and I felt sorry for him because his wife had left him but I still wanted to find out if his son was a murderer.

"Sure." He lumbered to his feet and took my empty cup. "Plenty more where that came from."

"Don't suppose you have a biscuit or cake to go with that?" I needed him to rummage around in the walk-in pantry, out of sight, so I could check the writing pad.

"Um…think I spotted some cupcakes with cream when I was looking for the donuts. They'd hit the spot."

"Sounds perfect." I screwed up my nose at his retreating back, shuddering as I imagined how sour the cream would taste if the cakes had been cooked by his long-departed wife.

As he disappeared into the pantry, I tiptoed across to the desk and tugged the writing pad out from under *Fred Flintstone's* dirty coffee ring. And there she was…*Betty Boop*…in all her sexy glory, big eyes, button nose, short dress, painted lips and legs that went up to her armpits.

My insides tangled like a ball of snarled rubber bands. Had Jason written the death threat to Harry on this writing pad? I lifted the pad so the light shone on the paper, checking for imprints. And there it was. Even without using a pencil, I could see in the bottom right-hand corner of the page where a piece had been torn off, the indentation of the words: HARRY YOU'RE DEAD.

The room swam. I looked up. Mr. Mc wasn't in the pantry any more. He was leaning against the sink, arms folded, watching me. His eyes hard. His mouth a slash of annoyance.

In my peripheral vision I could see the old dog gnawing on his right foot as though it didn't belong to him. The gnawing sounded like a rat chewing through wood.

"He took my Alice away from me," he said, his voice conversational, matter-of-fact. "She was mine. I loved her. He had every other woman in the dog show world dancing to his tune, but that wasn't enough for him. He wanted my woman too. I couldn't let him get away with that. I had to stop him."

Mouth dry, I felt my legs go floppier than over-cooked spaghetti and had to make a grab for the kitchen table to stay upright. I gasped. Held on tighter. So tight my knuckles went white. But I had to stay vigilant. Strong. And I needed workable legs to get me out from behind the table, through the kitchen door and into the semi-safety of the property outside.

It wasn't Jason McInerny who'd killed Harry Driscoll and the Mayor.

It was his father.

22

The room grew cold. I shivered. If I'd known I was going to come face to face with a murderer I'd have added a cardigan to my swirly white and pink author-signing dress before leaving home.

Mr. McInerny hadn't moved from where he was leaning against the kitchen sink, arms folded. But he was watching me. Watching every small movement of my body. Even the way my heart beat against my chest beneath the flimsy dress material.

I eyed the back door, the only way out. At least a dozen steps from where I sagged, holding myself up via the wooden table. The door was a sliding door made of glass. Wasn't locked, I could see a two-inch gap, meaning the door wasn't fully closed. Okay, so, if I wanted a chance of getting through that door and outside where I could hide and ring for help, I had to keep Mr. Mc. talking, distract him and get him off balance.

I looked back at Jason's dad, the nice man who'd lost his wife, the man who'd murdered two people and was currently contemplating on how to murder me and get away with it. My breath caught in my throat. He'd already worked that one out. While I'd been measuring the distance to my escape route, he'd chosen a shiny red apple from the fruit bowl, withdrew a large kitchen knife from the knife block and was slowly, menacingly, peeling the apple with the knife.

"You're a woman," he said, giving me a quick up and down, as if to check. "So, tell me this. What did Harry Driscoll have that I don't? Every woman fell for the man, including my Alice. What was it about him that was so magical?"

"Geez, how would I know?" Taken aback, I shuddered, pulled a yuk-triggered *eww* face. "Harry was old enough to be my father. I only ever nodded or said hello to the man when we passed at the shows."

"Go on, take a guess."

I watched how easily the peel slid off the apple. How sharply that kitchen knife had been honed. Okay, if talking about Harry's sexual expertise was a way to keep Mr. McInerny distracted, go for it, knock yourself out, I told myself. Loosening my grip on the table, I racked my brains for what would make one man more alluring in bed than another. "Um…could it be *length*?" I said with a shrug. Yeah, that was a good one.

His frown, aghast and fierce said I was wrong.

I dug deeper. "What about sexual flair? Positions? Foreplay?"

He growled.

"Okay, maybe the guy had charm? Charisma? Magnetism? Geez…I don't know. I only *write* romance – I don't live it."

He stopped peeling the apple and looked across at me, his eyes suddenly damp. "Charisma? That was the word Alice used when she packed her bags and told me she was leaving me. Said I had the charisma of old Caesar here." He glanced down at the comatose Chihuahua at his feet.

Oh dear…

"But if your wife left you over a month ago, why wait three weeks to kill Harry? Did it take that long to plot his demise?"

"No, no." He shook his head, wiped the dampness from his eyes with the fist holding the knife. "I didn't know Alice was on with that womanizing scumbag until the day before the dog show when I bumped into him at the local supermarket. Alice had been staying at a nearby B & B and I thought she just needed time, that she'd been inflicted with one of those stupid 'women's' problems – you know –

hormonal." He scowled at me as though I was the instigator of PMT, menopause, menstrual cycles and every other *women's complaint* since Eve chowed down on the apple. "I thought she'd come home when she realized how much she missed us, but Harry Driscoll actually had the gall to laugh at me that day, tell me I was a loser. He said he was *servicing* my wife at least six times a week and she couldn't get enough of him. *Servicing* – like she was a cow and he was a prized bull." He took a deep breath as though trying to steady himself and his eyes went dark, bleak. "And do you know the worst thing about all this?"

I shook my head.

"Harry didn't love my Alice. I think I could have forgiven him if he did, but she was just another notch in his cabinet full of trophies." His laugh sounded like nails on tin. "Why would he leave his wife and settle for *one* woman when he had a dozen or more fighting to get into bed with him?" His shoulders stiffened and his fingers, white from pressure, closed around the handle of the knife more tightly. "That's when I decided he had to go."

Wow…

"So," I said, eyes on the knife and hoping to steer him away from committing another murder. Mine. "What about the Mayor? Why did you decide to kill him?"

"Michael Hamilton-Davies?" He spat each word out like they tasted of bug slime. "That greedy toe-rag of a blackmailer said he had photos on his phone that showed me stabbing Harry." He let the last sliver of apple peel drop to the floor where the elderly Chihuahua, legs quivering, had already hacked up a pile of regurgitated peel. He ignored the latest addition and lurched back to his blanket-bed, where he buckled. "Had to get hold of his phone, didn't I?" Mr. Mc. continued. "Put a stop to the blackmail. I'd already paid the moneygrubbing slimeball fifty-thousand to keep him quiet but knew his demands wouldn't stop, so I banged him on the head and took the phone from his pocket. Didn't mean to kill him – just wanted his phone. Not my fault his pompous, I'm-a-Big-Shot head cracked like an egg when it connected with the shovel."

He took a bite of the apple but didn't return the knife to the knife block. Instead, the fingers of his right hand adjusted more comfortably around the handle.

I had to keep him talking but knew as soon as I ran out of topics that knife would probably be decorating my chest. "Was that your blood-stained shirt Jason was seen removing from the scene of the crime?" I tutted. "What father uses his own son as an accessory to murder? A crappy one – that's who."

He let out a sigh. Stopped chewing on the apple and a small frown indented his forehead. "Jason knows nothing of this. I told him I'd had a nose bleed and as it was a new shirt and I'd paid a bomb for it, could he take it home, spray the stain and soak the shirt in cold water. I wanted him right away from the showgrounds. Didn't want him questioned or involved when Harry's body was discovered." He lifted one eyebrow in query. "You've been talking to the two Miss Robertsons, haven't you?"

I nodded.

"Always were a couple of gossipy old witches."

I eyed the glass sliding door. If I waited any longer to make my move it might be too late. Mr. Mc. was leaning against the bench, seemingly deep in thought. Probably realizing his son might still be implicated in Harry's murder, by default. He *had* taken the blood-stained shirt from the crime scene.

As unobtrusively as possible, with the barest of movement, I let go of the table and flexed my knees, ready to throw myself across the room. If I didn't want to die in a pool of blood – all I had to do was get to the other side of that glass door.

But I didn't even reach the other side of the table before a sharp pain behind my right ear bent me over double. I let out a yelp. Saw stars. Felt the room spin, as the apple, minus its peel, slammed into the side of my head.

"If that had been my knife, you'd be dead." His voice was low, soft and menacing.

I blinked up at him, rubbed the area behind my right ear which was pulsing with pain. "Are you going to kill me, Mr. McInerny?"

Eyes unreadable, he stared at me. "What's the alternative?"

I could think of a hundred alternatives but although my brain was still working, my voice-box had decided to run up the white flag. I shook my head.

Eyes latched on mine, he leaned across the dog's bed of blankets, reaching for a replacement apple from the fruit bowl. Simultaneously, the grumbling Chihuahua, evidently uncomfortable lying on his back, began the arduous task of rolling over and staggering to his feet, just as the full weight of Mr. Mc's size twelve right foot landed square on the dog's front paw.

A high-pitched scream, more piercing than a banshee on the hunt, rent the air, threatening to explode every light bulb in the house. Mr. Mc. stumbled, peered down with an apologetic, 'I'm soorry, Caesar', and I shot through the doorway like the Ides of Hell and all their fire-breathing dragons were chasing me with well-sharpened pitchforks.

23

I needed somewhere safe to hide, to phone for help, before I became just another statistic languishing in a funeral parlor. As I ran, legs pumping wildly, every Mini, Standard, and Giant Schnauzer I passed in the dog yards ran up and down the wire, barking in excitement and blabbing my whereabouts to their owner. It was like he had them all programmed as his henchmen. I flipped a quick peep over my shoulder, but couldn't see my nemesis bursting through the doorway in hot pursuit, so I slowed to a jog, believing that might quieten the dogs down. Didn't happen. Every enclosure I passed, the occupants came racing across to the wire fence, bouncing, barking, eyes bright, tails wagging. Not only demanding I stop and chat, but signaling my location.

Up ahead, to the rear of the property, behind a high, badly-in-need-of-a-trim hedge, I spotted a galvanized iron shed. Looked like one of those garden sheds where you stored watering cans, mowers and snail bait. With one last peek over my shoulder – was that footsteps I could hear – I ducked behind the hedge and then barged through the shed's open doorway. Maybe I could lock the door from the inside and pray Mr. Mc. didn't have a spare key in his back pocket. Once inside, it didn't take long to discover that idea had holes in it. No key. Not even hooked on the rusty nail on the back of the door. Damn. In which case, I needed a weapon. Preferably one that would take out my knife-toting adversary with one blow. I was shaking so much by now, I doubted I'd have more than one worthwhile whack left in me.

Breathing like I'd run a marathon in cement-filled gumboots, I surfed the shed, hunting for a weapon. A powerful-looking lawn mower – too heavy to lift. An unopened bag of cement – ditto. Several ancient rat traps – although my pursuer fitted the description the traps were too small. And an old broom, so old, the head was completely hairless.

Not a lot to choose from.

But, as my Great Granny Teresa used to say, 'beggars can't be choosers', which translated in this situation to – 'if you're being chased by a man with a knife, a bald broom is better than a limp stick of celery.'

I snatched up the broom.

Clunk...

I froze. Was that a crunch of gravel outside the shed? Like a man's size twelves sneaking up on me? A man with knife-hand raised, eyes sparking death? My heart, already overstressed, thundered and leaped around in my chest like it was checking for the slightest opening so it could spring out and make a dash for the hills where it would hide in the safety of a Mumma kangaroo's joey-pouch. I took a step back, my fingers tightening around the handle of the broom, my body on high alert as I tried to stop the thumping of my heart from masking the tell-tale sounds of the hunter.

And that's when I spotted it. A small shed-door sized rusty key poking out from under an equally rusty rat-trap on the dusty bench.

Could my luck be changing? Was the Universe finally smiling down on me, or bent double, laughing hysterically at its devious joke to give me false hope? I snatched the key from the bench and slipped it in my pocket so I'd have both hands free for the upcoming attack.

Thud...

An unseen hand rattled the outside handle.

Like watching a snake preparing to strike, I stared at the door as it creaked open, inch by inch. I might be an introverted romance writer whose love life had no resemblance to those of my fictional characters, a scaredy-cat with inferiority hang-ups brought about by a too-strict Victorian-era childhood, but no way was I going down to this crazy, revenge-filled killer without a fight.

Hey, I had a new man in my life. I needed time to explore the possibility that Hudson was, as we romance writers say, 'The One'.

After sucking in a soundless breath to steady myself, I shifted both hands into a more balanced position around the splintery wooden broom handle and the moment a head, topped with tousled gray hair, appeared around the corner of the door, I lifted my weapon high in the air, imagined myself hitting a homer for the New York Yankees, and brought it down…

Thwack…

The last thing I heard, after the broom handle snapped, the gray-haired murderer went splat on his knees on the cement floor, and I slammed the shed door behind me, was a gurgling guttural, 'Uggh!'

Praying to all the Gods, both Biblical and Mythical, I hauled the rusty key from my pocket and, fingers fumbling, attempted to jam it into the keyhole. Please work. Please be the key to this shed and not to a long-forgotten letterbox, thrown out umpteen years ago when the McInernys replaced it with one shaped like a Giant Schnauzer.

At first a little reluctant, the key finally turned in the keyhole, just as the first loud thump sounded on the other side of the shed door.

"Let me out!"

As if.

The door shuddered and groaned as my captive indicated exactly what he thought of his incarceration. Oh. My. God. Not sure if the door would hold against his onslaught, I spun around with the intention of beating a hasty retreat to my car and slammed into the rock-solid body of a man wearing a black leather jacket, knee-high motor cycle boots and a look on his face that said, 'If that guy's hurt you, I'll feed him through the dog mincer!'

"H-Hudson?" My heart, which moments earlier had gone hunting for a Prozac, immediately bounced back into my chest and smiled broadly. It wasn't the knife-wielding Mr. McInerny, who'd somehow performed a Houdini act and escaped his prison, but the man I'd most want to be with on the back of a speeding Harley. Naked.

Both arms came around me, drawing me into his body. "You okay, Molly?"

I nodded into the comforting smell of soft black leather and that familiar fresh woodsy cologne that reminded me of Springtime in the forest, before gazing up into two worried blue eyes. Hudson Driscoll really cared about me. Me, Molly Gibson. Introverted romance writer, whose real-life love affairs so far had been akin to Pooh Bear's escapades with honey-bees.

He smiled down at me, I smiled back, and then I thought, *but how did Hudson know I was here?*

It took all of two seconds for the penny to drop. I jerked back, frowning. "How did you know I was at the McInerny's house? Are you psychic?" My frown deepened. "Or were you following–"

I got no further. His lips, warm, sweet and rather moreish, exactly as I remembered from our first kiss in front of Nathan's PI's office, closed over my mouth, effectively shutting me up.

What felt like ten but was probably only two minutes later, when we finally came up for air, he gently brushed a stray lock of hair from my cheek with one finger, but made no move to let me go. "Remember what I said earlier today about one and one making two?" His voice was sexy, hot, sort of rich and rumbly.

I might have answered, *yes*, but it could have been a moan.

"Well, you, Molly Gibson, said you were at a bakery in Two Wells when I rang – a hop, step and jump from the McInerny's Schnauzer Stud. And then, when I rang Dana to get an update, she told me about Jason's blood-stained shirt." He raised his eyebrows at me. Two very sexy eyebrows, I might add. Then, shook his head. "So, I figured that meant you were currently at the McInerny's house digging yourself into a whole lot of trouble."

"Yeah, turned out to be quite a big hole," I admitted as Hudson brushed his warm lips across my cheek and nibbled down my neck. I took a deep breath, reluctantly dragged my brain out of the foggy love-cloud surrounding me and back into the reality of our present situation. "But it wasn't Jason who murdered your father and the Mayor," I told him. "It was Mr. McInerny. He's the one locked in the shed, and he's armed with a kitchen knife." I pulled my phone from my back pocket. "Guess I'd better ring the police."

"What am I? Chopped liver? I *am* the police." Hudson's warm lips nuzzled my forehead. "But as I'm not on this case due to that monster in the shed being my father's murderer, I've already rung for backup."

Loose stones rattled on the path behind us.

I swung around, ready to take on the next combatant with my bare hands – and maybe a lights-out left hook from Hudson, you know, just to back me up.

How's that for having a spine, Great Granny Teresa.

"Molly! Molly! Oh, my God, you're not dead!"

I grinned. It was Abi, hair standing on end, as though she'd been running her fingers through in frustration – or fear. "Definitely not dead, Abs," I told her, "but shakier than a ready-to-eat jelly." I stepped reluctantly out of Hudson's arms and moved toward my best friend, my shaky legs threatening to dump me on the path. I wasn't sure if that was due to the knife-wielding murderer banging on the shed door three feet away or the effect of Hudson's kisses.

I'll stick with the latter.

"We couldn't find you inside the house and panicked." Abi's bear-hug almost lifted me off the ground.

I smiled into her shoulder. "Who's we?"

"The other *Gumshoe Chick*, of course." Dana, wielding a baseball bat, strode up the path toward us. She tipped her head in the direction of the shed door which was close to losing the battle. "Who the heck's making that awful ruckus?"

"Mr. McInerny."

"And he's locked in his own shed because…?"

I quickly filled my two friends in on the reason I'd detained the owner of the property. Told them Jason wasn't the murderer, it was his father who'd avenged his wife's infidelity. By the time I'd finished, two police cars had screeched to a halt outside the house, discharging Detective Lightfoot and half a dozen gun-toting police officers who streamed around the back of the house.

Events moved quickly from there.

Five officers surrounded the garden shed, one calling out to McInerny to lay down his weapon and lie flat on the ground, face first, as they were coming in. The other constable, a poker-faced policewoman, shoulders dipped in starch, requested our statement be given inside the house, while Detective Lightfoot, dressed in a smart pale blue suit, matching tie and Italian loafers, took Hudson to one side.

I could see Lightfoot talking quietly, one arm around Hudson's shoulders and my approval of the detective went up ten notches. This had to be hard for Hudson, confronting his father's murderer. Yet, he still managed to wave over his shoulder at me as I followed the policewoman toward the house and to call out, 'Okay if I pick you up at nine tonight?'

I turned and sent him an answering grin.

Was the Pope Catholic?

Could Elvis sing?

Did Scotsmen feel the cold in their nether regions when they donned their kilts?

As we trotted behind the policewoman, Dana hitched one arm through mine while Abi claimed the other. A comforting warmth spread through me replacing the chill brought on by McInerny's deadly threats.

Hey, I had two amazing friends who were always there for me, even when there was a bad guy on the loose. Add to that, I'd somehow hitched up with a romance hero far better than I could have ever thought up myself.

And the icing on the cake…

This biker-slash-cop *really* liked me.

Could life get any better than that?

Dear Readers

FOR THE LOVE OF DOGS is the second book in my new series, the *Gumshoe Chick Mysteries,* this time starring romance writer, Molly. There's three *Chicks* – Abigail Truelove, Molly Gibson and Dana Fox. All dog-show competitors. All 28-year-old Nancy-Drew-wannabees. All owners of pampered pooches. If you've enjoyed reading this why not go back to wherever you bought this book from and leave an honest review? Reviews are like dessert for us authors. In fact, they are part of what keeps me writing – knowing you've spent time with the characters I created, dressed up and injected with life. Especially for you.

If you'd like to catch up with me on Facebook, go to: https://facebook.com/JuneWhyteBooks.

Or to check out my website, go here: www.junewhytebooks.com

I'd also like to acknowledge and thank those who have helped me in my writing journey. My beta readers, Nancy, June K and Bev – couldn't do without you. My forever friends, Robyn and Wendy – I know I can always whip off an email with a question or ask for a second opinion and it will be answered with a smile. And Traci Andrighetti, USA bestselling author of the *Franki Amato mysteries,* whose suggestions and edits have seen me grow as an author.

And for those who haven't yet read, GONE TO THE DOGS, the first book in the *Gumshoe Chicks* Mysteries, I've included the first chapter, just for you.

Thank you,
June Whyte

GONE TO THE DOGS
CHAPTER 1

My name is Abigail Truelove and my life changed the day I discovered Petra Sullivan, my nemesis, was sleeping with the show judge.

The Ladies Kennel-Club was staging its Annual Championship dog show at the Royal Adelaide Showground and over the last four hours, two hundred or more competitors had stacked, primed, and shown off their dog's attributes to the presiding judges.

It was now down to the group finalists. Seven dogs, battling it out for the coveted Best in Show award. And as my smooth-haired dachshund, *Tempestuous Dawn* had won Best in Hound Group, I stood in the middle of the line-up, my dog stacked, alert, and ready.

An order from the judge sent the winner of the Gundog Group, the Honorable Lady Felicity Taylor, into instant action. She lifted her three chins high in the air and set off around the ring with her jet-black cocker spaniel in tow. God, that dog could move. Pity it didn't have a brain in its head. Not that it mattered. When it came to Best in Show material, surface beauty was all that counted.

Since joining the competitive show ranks, I'd learned that dog shows were akin to a battle ground. Like hard-fought wars, strategies to win that coveted Best in Show sash were planned with precision and dedication. Hours on the treadmill to keep up the dog's muscle-tone. Marathon do-overs with clippers, brushes and expensive beauty products. Secret diets passed down through generations of show families.

I'd inherited *Tempestuous Dawn* (aka Chloe, the most gorgeous and lovable dachshund on this earth) a year ago when my favorite relative, Aunt Tilly, died of a heart attack while kayaking in the North of Queensland. Not having children of her own, she also left me *Pampered Pooch,* an exclusive doggy boutique that sold designer-brand products on the High Street. At the time, my boyfriend, Luke, although happy with the money generated from the boutique, wasn't too keen on the canine edition to our family. He complained about the time I spent with the 'bloody dog' and pretended to be allergic to the minutest amount of dog hair left on the sofa. Right from the start, he'd advocated selling Chloe; said we'd get big bucks for the dog. But it wasn't going to happen. One – Aunt Tilly would rise up her from the grave if I dared put *Tempestuous Dawn* on the market. And two – I fell head over heels in love with the quirky little dog and decided I'd continue showing her. After all, this dog was a near-perfect specimen of the breed and under Aunt Tilly's expert handling had previously won Best in Show in every state of Australia.

Not that I'd enjoyed Aunt Tilly's success. At the first five shows I'd entered, Chloe had bombed. Dramatically. She hadn't even won her breed class.

But today, with the sound of crated dogs yapping from inside the pavilion and the overpowering scent of whichever new beauty product Lady Felicity had doused both herself and her cocker-spaniel, *Mein Freund Merry Widow*, I was determined to give it my best shot.

Lady Felicity, nose in the air, completed two laps of the ring and moved back into line with the other finalists. A total professional, she immediately presented her dog to the judge, head up, tail straight and four legs in perfect alignment. A twenty-year doyen of the game, the woman's show-ring skills and professional attire always went a long way towards collecting Best in Show ribbons.

While realigning Chloe's left ear so it sat in perfect placement to her right ear, I noticed my best friend Molly Gibson plucking nervously at the number tag pinned to her shirt. Molly had only joined the show dog ranks to keep me company. And although Busta, her smooth-coated Fox Terrier, absolutely loved to show off in the ring, Molly was happier in the background, helping to run the shows. This was the first time Busta had won Best Terrier in Group and by the way Molly was chewing on her fingernails, she wouldn't be opening any tricky butter-pats in the near future.

"Number twenty-six, lady with the smooth-haired dachshund, I'd like to see your dog's paces please." The judge, an older guy with a cowlick and shoes that were a little run down at the heels, nodded his head at me.

Again? God, this judge was taking more time to make up his mind than a group of politicians debating Climate Change.

I sucked in a quick steadying breath. "Okay, my love, let's show them what you can do." With a slight tug on Chloe's lead I stepped out of the line-up. Having already won Champion of Breed and Champion Hound, if I could keep Chloe's attention a little longer, she had a good chance of winning Best in Show.

Tempestuous Dawn floated across the ground with me powering along beside her, puffing like the little-engine-that-could. Understandable, considering I'd scarfed an entire block of Rocky Road chocolate, plus a large packet of M&Ms before entering the ring – show-nerves – so by the time we moved back into line, the sweat welling on my face was doing a pretty good job of removing my makeup.

But the moment we came to a halt, Chloe began to sag.

"No, no, no. Only a couple more minutes," I whispered, trying valiantly to keep her stumpy little legs from folding, while silently willing the judge to get his ass into gear and make a decision.

"Sorreee…I got held up in the Little Girls Room."

I blinked in surprise as the shark of the show-world, Petra Sullivan, bee-stung lips the color of old plasma, and hot pink jeans so tight you could define every delineation of her *hoo-ha*, sashayed into the show-ring, her overweight pug, the dubious winner of the Toy Group, dragging along behind her.

"Hey, you can't waltz in here now, you're too late!" I hissed through gritted teeth as Petra stopped in front of me to adjust one of her overflowing boobs.

How did she even get past the steward at the gate?

Petra's grin was so smarmy it would curdle yoghurt. She gave a tiny shoulder-shrug in response, then proceeded to push her way into first-cab-off-the-rank position at the top of the line-up. All the while ignoring the snorts of anger from the handlers of the other six Group winners.

Surely, Mr. Oliver Hutchins, who purported to have judged at big shows in both England and America, would order the gate-crasher out of the ring. This class had been in progress for half an hour. The judge was on the brink of announcing his winner. No way could a contestant enter the ring and be judged once a class was in action.

The rules were in black and white.

All eyes swiveled from Perky Petra to Mr. Procrastination. All waiting in anticipation for the interloper to be tossed out on her well-defined derriere. But nothing happened. Not a crumb of censure passed the esteemed judge's lips. No steward came to drag Petra out of the ring by her ultra-long false eyelashes. Instead, Oliver T. Hutchins grew an inch or two taller, sucked in his stomach and straightened his bow-tie. All the while beaming at the latest competitor as though she was a double decker chocolate-swirl ice-cream and he couldn't wait to lick her.

Had he been stalling? Waiting for Petra to enter the ring? Was that why he'd been taking so long to announce his winner?

At first, when the whispers skittered along the line-up that Petra was *doing* the judge, I couldn't believe it. That is, until Petra threw a little finger wave in the direction of Mr. Easily-Swayed and he answered with a suggestive lick of his lips and an almost imperceptible pelvic thrust. *A pelvic thrust?* At his age? I could feel the ire churning around in my chest, escalating with every spin and preparing to explode via my mouth with a few well-chosen, but completely unladylike words. Pitched at a very high volume. Hey, I'd been the bunny who'd spent hours on the phone with this guy as a representative of the Ladies Kennel Club. I'd been the one who'd pleaded and offered him more money than our club could afford to pay for his services.

Silly me…I'd got it wrong.

I'd stroked the guy's ego while Petra stroked his whatnot.

As I watched the judge swagger across the ring, his eyes lasering in on the pair of double D's escaping from the front of Petra's low-cut blouse, I knew we'd missed the boat.

Chloe must have sensed it too. Weary of all this standing around looking suave and beautiful, she decided it was way past her nap time. She dug several pivots out of the grass, turned three times on the spot, curled up in a ball and promptly fell sleep.

I didn't bother waking her. What was the point? Even considered the merits of joining her.

The judge, after sending Petra and *Princess Sauvignon of Glenville* for one measly lap of the ring, pulled the fat little pug out of the line-up and presented Petra with a trophy and the coveted multi-colored Best in Show sash.

Unbelievable.

The moment Petra exited the ring, the other six Group winners rounded on her. For a split second, I actually felt sorry for the woman. But only for a split second.

"You conniving little tart!" Stephen Channing, owner of the Non-Sporting Group winner, a beautifully trimmed-and-primped-to-within-an-inch-of-its-life apricot Standard Poodle, *Supreme Champion Windswept Fly By Me*, who'd won more Best in Show ribbons than most dogs had breakfasts, got right up into her face. His gold medallion, ear rings and matching necklace vibrating with his anger. "You bitch! You slept with him, didn't you?"

Petra wrinkled her nose. "Back up, Stevie. Your breath smells like you've been sucking on some guy's...dirty socks."

"Stone the flamin' crows!" snarled Wild Bill Hooter, the bearded winner of the Working Dog group. "Stephen's right. You're nothing but a tart!" He spat a lump of phlegm in Petra's direction, completely ignoring his Border Collie who was attempting to hump Petra's pug.

"*I'm* lodging a formal complaint to the committee." Lady Felicity snatched up her Cocker Spaniel who was also showing interest in Petra's pop-eyed pug and stormed off in the direction of the Secretary's office.

The accusations fell on deaf ears.

Petra, all smiles, shimmied a path through the angry contestants, all the while flapping her Best in Show ribbon in our faces, like a matador waving a red cape at a bull.

"What I don't understand is how you could *do* that, Petra? How you could climb into bed with a guy old enough to be your father, a guy you don't even know – just to win a ribbon?" That was Molly, my best friend. Of course, Molly's views on sex were a little out-dated. Like a marriage certificate in full view on the bed-side table and even then, nothing more erotic than the missionary position while lying back and *doing it for England.*

Over the years, I'd tried to drag my friend into the 21st Century, but it was a hard-uphill slog. Probably because Molly's parents died in a car crash when she was four and she'd been brought up by her strict Great-Granny Teresa, whose archaic ideas of carnality meant the actual word *sex* hadn't been invented yet.

There was a scuffle at my feet. I looked down and let out a laugh. Busta, Molly's exuberant Fox Terrier knew *exactly* what the word sex meant. He was going hammer-and-tongs on top of *Princess Sauvignon of Glenville* like it was Christmas morning and Santa had left the little pug under the tree, all boxed and gift-wrapped, just for him.

Petra's laugh was breathy, almost a snigger. "You're *so* naïve, Molly. It's almost as if you never left high school."

"But you didn't answer her question," I said, bending to help my friend extricate Busta from his carnal bliss before facing up to Petra.

"That's easy. I *adore* sex." Petra flicked her shoulder-length bottle-blonde hair over her shoulder as if that explained everything. "And if being horny gets me what I want in life, why not?"

I shoved Busta into Molly's arms and turned back to Petra. "Even if it means cheating?"

"Prove it."

"I intend to."

Petra barked out a laugh. "Oh, Abi, do you honestly believe Mr. Please-Pass-the-Viagra would admit to having sex in return for favours rendered. If so, you're as delusional as your weird friend." She eyed the accusing faces around her, all hanging on to her every word. "You know, if I divulged the names of all the guys I've slept with – just this month – at least *one* of you losers would be booting your other-half out of the cosy love-nest." As she spoke, her hard eyes, glinting with malice, zeroed in on me.

"What do you mean?" My voice came out strangled, as though a lump the size of a tennis ball had lodged in my throat. "What are you implying?"

Molly touched my arm. "Come on, Abi, she's just winding you up."

"I'm *implying* nothing." Petra stepped closer, a smirk thickening her cosmetically full-blown lips. "All I'm saying is *maybe* some men prefer to suck on juicy watermelons instead of–" she tipped her head forward and blatantly studied my chest. "–sour little lemons? And *maybe* some men look forward to fireworks in bed, instead of damp squibs."

I shrugged off Molly's restraining hand, a bitter taste of bile flooding my mouth. Was Luke really having it off with Petra? Was that why he seemed a little preoccupied, lately? Accusing me of not trusting him? Telling me I was too clingy?

Well, if this was a test – he'd failed miserably. It proved I was right all along not to trust him.

Or was Petra lying?

"If I find out you've been in bed with Luke," I growled, grabbing hold of Petra's arm and swinging her around, forcibly holding back from planting a fist into that smirking face. "I'll dice you into little pieces and feed you to the sea-gulls."

"Oh, dear, always so dramatic." Petra pulled away and laughed. "If it helps, *darling*, sex means nothing to me. It's just a bit of fun. Like scratching an itch."

My nails bit into my palms as my fists tightened.

"Come on, Abi, don't let her get to you," Molly broke in, dragging me away, her face pale. I took my eyes off Petra long enough to glance across at my best friend. Molly looked upset. Sick. She had that haunted expression on her face – the one that said, '*Oh, God, it looks like a fight…and I'm so not into fisticuffs or hair-pulling because I'll be the one who ends up in hospital or paying for a new hairstyle to cover the gaps in my hair.*'

"But Petra slept with Luke."

"She's winding you up. Can't you see that? No way would Luke cheat on you." Molly's grip on my arm tightened. "Especially with a woman who treats sex like an Extreme Olympic Sport. Luke loves you."

All the red-hot anger crashing around inside my chest suddenly abated and dribbled away. "Does he?" I could hear the wobble in my voice. "That's the problem, Molly. I'm not so sure he does."

Dear Readers

GONE TO THE DOGS is the first book in my new series, the *Gumshoe Chick Mysteries*. There are three *Chicks* – Abigail Truelove, Molly Gibson and Dana Fox. All dog-show competitors. All 28-year-old Nancy-Drew-wannabees. All owners of pampered pooches. If you've enjoyed reading GONE TO THE DOGS, why not pop over to Amazon, or whichever online store you bought this book from and leave an honest review? Reviews are like dessert for authors. In fact, they are part of what keeps me writing – knowing you've spent time with the characters I created, dressed up and injected with life. Especially for you.

www.junewhytebooks.com.

I'd also like to acknowledge and thank those who have helped me in my writing journey. My beta readers, Nancy, June K and Bev – couldn't do without you. My forever friends, Robyn and Wendy – I know I can always whip off an email with a question or ask for a second opinion and it will be answered with a smile. And Traci Andrighetti, USA bestselling author of the *Franki Amato Mysteries*, whose suggestions and edits made this book the best it could be.

Thank you,
June Whyte

Gone to the Dogs

1

My name is Abigail Truelove and my life changed the day I discovered Petra Sullivan, my nemesis, was sleeping with the show judge.

The Ladies Kennel-Club was staging its Annual Championship dog show at the Royal Adelaide Showground and over the last four hours, two hundred or more competitors had stacked, primed, and shown off their dog's attributes to the presiding judges.

It was now down to the group finalists. Seven dogs, battling it out for the coveted Best in Show award. And as my smooth-haired dachshund, *Tempestuous Dawn* had won Best in Hound Group, I stood in the middle of the line-up, my dog stacked, alert, and ready.

An order from the judge sent the winner of the Gundog Group, the Honorable Lady Felicity Taylor, into instant action. She lifted her three chins high in the air and set off around the ring with her jet-black cocker spaniel in tow. God, that dog could move. Pity it didn't have a brain in its head. Not that it mattered. When it came to Best in Show material, surface beauty was all that counted.

Since joining the competitive show ranks, I'd learned that dog shows were akin to a battle ground. Like hard-fought wars, strategies to win that coveted Best in Show sash were planned with precision and dedication. Hours on the treadmill to keep up the dog's muscle-tone. Marathon do-overs with clippers, brushes and expensive beauty products. Secret diets passed down through generations of show families.

I'd inherited *Tempestuous Dawn* (aka Chloe, the most gorgeous and lovable dachshund on this earth) a year ago when my favorite relative, Aunt Tilly, died of a heart attack while kayaking in the North of Queensland. Not having children of her own, she also left me *Pampered Pooch,* an exclusive doggy boutique that sold designer-brand products on the High Street. At the time, my boyfriend, Luke, although happy with the money generated from the boutique, wasn't too keen on the canine edition to our family. He complained about the time I spent with the 'bloody dog' and pretended to be allergic to the minutest amount of dog hair left on the sofa. Right from the start, he'd advocated selling Chloe; said we'd get big bucks for the dog. But it wasn't going to happen. One – Aunt Tilly would rise up her from the grave if I dared put *Tempestuous Dawn* on the market. And two – I fell head over heels in love with the quirky little dog and decided I'd continue showing her. After all, this dog was a near-perfect specimen of the breed and under Aunt Tilly's expert handling had previously won Best in Show in every state of Australia.

Not that I'd enjoyed Aunt Tilly's success. At the first five shows I'd entered, Chloe had bombed. Dramatically. She hadn't even won her breed class.

But today, with the sound of crated dogs yapping from inside the pavilion and the overpowering scent of whichever new beauty product Lady Felicity had doused both herself and her cocker-spaniel, *Mein Freund Merry Widow*, I was determined to give it my best shot.

Lady Felicity, nose in the air, completed two laps of the ring and moved back into line with the other finalists. A total professional, she immediately presented her dog to the judge, head up, tail straight and four legs in perfect alignment. A twenty-year doyen of the game, the woman's show-ring skills and professional attire always went a long way towards collecting Best in Show ribbons.

While realigning Chloe's left ear so it sat in perfect placement to her right ear, I noticed my best friend Molly Gibson plucking nervously at the number tag pinned to her shirt. Molly had only joined the show dog ranks to keep me company. And although Busta, her smooth-coated Fox Terrier, absolutely loved to show off in the ring, Molly was happier in the background, helping to run the shows. This was the first time Busta had won Best Terrier in Group and by the way Molly was chewing on her fingernails, she wouldn't be opening any tricky butter-pats in the near future.

"Number twenty-six, lady with the smooth-haired dachshund, I'd like to see your dog's paces please." The judge, an older guy with a cowlick and shoes that were a little run down at the heels, nodded his head at me.

Again? God, this judge was taking more time to make up his mind than a group of politicians debating Climate Change.

I sucked in a quick steadying breath. "Okay, my love, let's show them what you can do." With a slight tug on Chloe's lead I stepped out of the line-up. Having already won Champion of Breed and Champion Hound, if I could keep Chloe's attention a little longer, she had a good chance of winning Best in Show.

Tempestuous Dawn floated across the ground with me powering along beside her, puffing like the little-engine-that-could. Understandable, considering I'd scarfed an entire block of Rocky Road chocolate, plus a large packet of M&Ms before entering the ring – show-nerves – so by the time we moved back into line, the sweat welling on my face was doing a pretty good job of removing my makeup.

But the moment we came to a halt, Chloe began to sag.

"No, no, no. Only a couple more minutes," I whispered, trying valiantly to keep her stumpy little legs from folding, while silently willing the judge to get his ass into gear and make a decision.

"Sorreee…I got held up in the Little Girls Room."

I blinked in surprise as the shark of the show-world, Petra Sullivan, bee-stung lips the color of old plasma, and hot pink jeans so tight you could define every delineation of her *hoo-ha*, sashayed into the show-ring, her overweight pug, the dubious winner of the Toy Group, dragging along behind her.

"Hey, you can't waltz in here now, you're too late!" I hissed through gritted teeth as Petra stopped in front of me to adjust one of her overflowing boobs.

How did she even get past the steward at the gate?

Petra's grin was so smarmy it would curdle yoghurt. She gave a tiny shoulder-shrug in response, then proceeded to push her way into first-cab-off-the-rank position at the top of the line-up. All the while ignoring the snorts of anger from the handlers of the other six Group winners.

Surely, Mr. Oliver Hutchins, who purported to have judged at big shows in both England and America, would order the gate-crasher out of the ring. This class had been in progress for half an hour. The judge was on the brink of announcing his winner. No way could a contestant enter the ring and be judged once a class was in action.

The rules were in black and white.

All eyes swiveled from Perky Petra to Mr. Procrastination. All waiting in anticipation for the interloper to be tossed out on her well-defined derriere. But nothing happened. Not a crumb of censure passed the esteemed judge's lips. No steward came to drag Petra out of the ring by her ultra-long false eyelashes. Instead, Oliver T. Hutchins grew an inch or two taller, sucked in his stomach and straightened his bow-tie. All the while beaming at the latest competitor as though she was a double decker chocolate-swirl ice-cream and he couldn't wait to lick her.

Had he been stalling? Waiting for Petra to enter the ring? Was that why he'd been taking so long to announce his winner?

At first, when the whispers skittered along the line-up that Petra was *doing* the judge, I couldn't believe it. That is, until Petra threw a little finger wave in the direction of Mr. Easily-Swayed and he answered with a suggestive lick of his lips and an almost imperceptible pelvic thrust. *A pelvic thrust?* At his age? I could feel the ire churning around in my chest, escalating with every spin and preparing to explode via my mouth with a few well-chosen, but completely unladylike words. Pitched at a very high volume. Hey, I'd been the bunny who'd spent hours on the phone with this guy as a representative of the Ladies Kennel Club. I'd been the one who'd pleaded and offered him more money than our club could afford to pay for his services.

Silly me…I'd got it wrong.

I'd stroked the guy's ego while Petra stroked his whatnot.

As I watched the judge swagger across the ring, his eyes lasering in on the pair of double D's escaping from the front of Petra's low-cut blouse, I knew we'd missed the boat.

Chloe must have sensed it too. Weary of all this standing around looking suave and beautiful, she decided it was way past her nap time. She dug several pivots out of the grass, turned three times on the spot, curled up in a ball and promptly fell sleep.

I didn't bother waking her. What was the point? Even considered the merits of joining her.

The judge, after sending Petra and *Princess Sauvignon of Glenville* for one measly lap of the ring, pulled the fat little pug out of the line-up and presented Petra with a trophy and the coveted multi-colored Best in Show sash.

Unbelievable.

The moment Petra exited the ring, the other six Group winners rounded on her. For a split second, I actually felt sorry for the woman. But only for a split second.

"You conniving little tart!" Steven Channing, owner of the Non-Sporting Group winner, a beautifully trimmed-and-primped-to-within-an-inch-of-its-life apricot Standard Poodle, *Supreme Champion Windswept Fly By Me*, who'd won more Best in Show ribbons than most dogs had breakfasts, got right up into her face. His gold medallion, ear rings and matching necklace vibrating with his anger. "You bitch! You slept with him, didn't you?"

Petra wrinkled her nose. "Back up, Stevie. Your breath smells like you've been sucking on some guy's…dirty socks."

"Stone the flamin' crows!" snarled Wild Bill Hooter, the bearded winner of the Working Dog group. "Stephen's right. You're nothing but a tart!" He spat a lump of phlegm in Petra's direction, completely ignoring his Border Collie who was attempting to hump Petra's pug.

"*I'm* lodging a formal complaint to the committee." Lady Felicity snatched up her Cocker Spaniel who was also showing interest in Petra's pop-eyed pug and stormed off in the direction of the Secretary's office.

The accusations fell on deaf ears.

Petra, all smiles, shimmied a path through the angry contestants, all the while flapping her Best in Show ribbon in our faces, like a matador waving a red cape at a bull.

"What I don't understand is how you could *do* that, Petra? How you could climb into bed with a guy old enough to be your father, a guy you don't even know – just to win a ribbon?" That was Molly, my best friend. Of course, Molly's views on sex were a little out-dated. Like a marriage certificate in full view on the bed-side table and even then, nothing more erotic than the missionary position while lying back and *doing it for England.*

Over the years, I'd tried to drag my friend into the 21st Century, but it was a hard-uphill slog. Probably because Molly's parents died in a car crash when she was four and she'd been brought up by her strict Great-Granny Teresa, whose archaic ideas of carnality meant the actual word *sex* hadn't been invented yet.

There was a scuffle at my feet. I looked down and let out a laugh. Busta, Molly's exuberant Fox Terrier knew *exactly* what the word sex meant. He was going hammer-and-tongs on top of *Princess Sauvignon of Glenville* like it was Christmas morning and Santa had left the little pug under the tree, all boxed and gift-wrapped, just for him.

Petra's laugh was breathy, almost a snigger. "You're *so* naïve, Molly. It's almost as if you never left high school."

"But you didn't answer her question," I said, bending to help my friend extricate Busta from his carnal bliss before facing up to Petra.

"That's easy. I *adore* sex." Petra flicked her shoulder-length bottle-blonde hair over her shoulder as if that explained everything. "And if being horny gets me what I want in life, why not?"

I shoved Busta into Molly's arms and turned back to Petra. "Even if it means cheating?"

"Prove it."

"I intend to."

Petra barked out a laugh. "Oh, Abi, do you honestly believe Mr. Please-Pass-the-Viagra would admit to having sex in return for favours rendered. If so, you're as delusional as your weird friend." She eyed the accusing faces around her, all hanging on to her every word. "You know, if I divulged the names of all the guys I've slept with – just this month – at least *one* of you losers would be booting your other-half out of the cosy love-nest." As she spoke, her hard eyes, glinting with malice, zeroed in on me.

"What do you mean?" My voice came out strangled, as though a lump the size of a tennis ball had lodged in my throat. "What are you implying?"

Molly touched my arm. "Come on, Abi, she's just winding you up."

"I'm *implying* nothing." Petra stepped closer, a smirk thickening her cosmetically full-blown lips. "All I'm saying is *maybe* some men prefer to suck on juicy watermelons instead of–" she tipped her head forward and blatantly studied my chest. "–sour little lemons? And *maybe* some men look forward to fireworks in bed, instead of damp squibs."

I shrugged off Molly's restraining hand, a bitter taste of bile flooding my mouth. Was Luke really having it off with Petra? Was that why he seemed a little preoccupied, lately? Accusing me of not trusting him? Telling me I was too clingy?

Well, if this was a test – he'd failed miserably. It proved I was right all along not to trust him.

Or was Petra lying?

"If I find out you've been in bed with Luke," I growled, grabbing hold of Petra's arm and swinging her around, forcibly holding back from planting a fist into that smirking face. "I'll dice you into little pieces and feed you to the sea-gulls."

"Oh, dear, always so dramatic." Petra pulled away and laughed. "If it helps, *darling*, sex means nothing to me. It's just a bit of fun. Like scratching an itch."

My nails bit into my palms as my fists tightened.

"Come on, Abi, don't let her get to you," Molly broke in, dragging me away, her face pale. I took my eyes off Petra long enough to glance across at my best friend. Molly looked upset. Sick. She had that haunted expression on her face – the one that said, '*Oh, God, it looks like a fight…and I'm so not into fisticuffs or hair-pulling because I'll be the one who ends up in hospital or paying for a new hairstyle to cover the gaps in my hair.*'

"But Petra slept with Luke."

"She's winding you up. Can't you see that? No way would Luke cheat on you." Molly's grip on my arm tightened. "Especially with a woman who treats sex like an Extreme Olympic Sport. Luke loves you."

All the red-hot anger crashing around inside my chest suddenly abated and dribbled away. "Does he?" I could hear the wobble in my voice. "That's the problem, Molly. I'm not so sure he does."